THE BEAST
& HIS
BEAUTY

WILLOW WINTERS
WALL STREET JOURNAL & USA TODAY BESTSELLING AUTHOR

From USA Today Best Selling author Willow Winters comes a retelling of the Fairytale Fantasy.

They don't go to the brick wall. No one in the village does. Ever since I was a little girl, everyone has warned me not to go or even to look at it. And if you happen to find yourself close to the wall, run as fast and as far away as you can. The magic from the beast creeps beyond the wall, but not by much.

No one who values their life approaches the enchanted area, let alone searches out the gate. Everyone is sure not to provoke the enchanted area. Those who do, don't come back to tell their tales.
The magic is dark. And it's all from the beast.

For the last 19 years of my life, I've heard the tales and been warned to stay away. The thing is though, I'm not a very good listener. I got lost in the magic. He scented me. He claimed me with a bite on my neck. And I ran. Quickly and with a new terror racing in my heart. I swore I would never return. I would not trust the magic and allow it to entrance me again. I would not risk being caught in the hands of the Beast again.

But that was months ago and I miss the magic. Not only that, but I dream of the beast. It's not a dream I'd admit to out loud, but it's a dream I'd like to see come true.

THE PRINCE
&
ELLE

CHAPTER 1

ELLE

They don't go to the brick wall. No one in the village does. Since I was a little girl, everyone has warned me not to go to it or even to look at it. And if you happen to find yourself close to the wall, run as fast and as far away as you can. The magic from the beast creeps beyond the wall, but not by much.

The wall itself is miles long and so high that you can hardly see the castle beyond it. There's a single entrance, an iron gate somewhere in the woods, that you have to use to get past the wall, if for some reason you want to go to the castle. Of course no one does. No one who values their life approaches the enchanted area, let alone searches out the gate. You can easily see the wall from dirt roads in the village. Although some may pass it, they keep their eyes away, their heads bowed, and silently and quickly pass. Everyone is sure not to provoke the enchanted area. Those who do, don't come back to tell their tales.

The magic is dark. And it's all due to the beast.

Decades ago, a witch came and delivered the beast to the prince. Within hours, the sky grew dark as the witch's storm approached. The prince and all who resided in the castle fled. Dark witches are rare and often dealt with quickly and severely by their own kind. But the prince was not lucky enough to have an enchantress to aid him and his people. He offered himself in exchange for the safety of the village. And the witch greedily accepted. She fed him to the beast and laughed wickedly in triumph.

Her evil reign was short-lived. It took only two days for the witches to hear of what their sister had done. Once they'd learned, they came immediately and imprisoned the witch with bindings of magic then lit her aflame.

But the damage had already been done.

The sorceress could not bring back the prince, and the beast could not leave so long as the enchantment lasted. She promised a day would come when the curse would be broken, and she quickly left taking what little hope the people had with her. With the sorceress gone, the beast was left to reign. A darkness descended over the castle and the mist remained.

At least that's what we're told. Of course the beast does not come past the wall. They say he used to, that he tried to rule. But the people rose against him. Outside the walls, the magic is weaker, and the beast could not defend himself against the people. He retreated to the castle, beaten and badly wounded. Foolishly, some thought they'd be able to end the beast within the castle walls. They stormed his estate armed with their weapons. The men and even a few of the women went to crucify the beast. They say the screams could be heard for hours as he slaughtered and tortured the trespassers. Only the women came back to tell of the massacre.

For the last nineteen years of my life, I've heard these tales and been warned to stay away. The thing is though, I'm not a very good listener. So while no one else was interested in exploring the enchanted area, I was obsessed with it. Although I'd never seen the gate nor heard or seen the beast, I'd witnessed the swirls of darkness that move through the mist as I crossed the dirt roads. I didn't bother to hide my intrigue and maybe that pleased the magic because I'd often be rewarded with melodic songs from the forest as I gazed along the bewitched wall.

For months, I'd wander a bit into the forest and lean against the trees. I'd watch as flowers picked themselves up and floated toward me until the wind blew them just beyond my grasp and they disappeared behind the wall. The vines that grew along the wall would twine with one another and travel through the forest.

I feared the vines the most because they often came toward me, and I wasn't sure if it was due to curiosity or if the vines had intentions of their own. Once, when I was enthralled by a tree that moved its boughs for the squirrels as they barreled by each other in their playful manner, I didn't notice the vines. I didn't see them weaving together to form a rope. I didn't notice as they crawled along the dirt floor of the forest toward me. I didn't even feel them as they wrapped around my ankle. Not until they tugged me toward them.

My heart stopped beating and I screamed in terror. As soon as the sound escaped my lips, I regretted my reaction. The forest went still and everything retreated, including the vines. In a frightened blink all the magic had left. I apologized profusely and willed the forest to entertain me with its magic, but to no avail. I walked to where the vines laid on the dirt and gently picked them up, stroking the dark green leaves. They did not respond.

I was genuinely sorry that I'd frightened the magic, and I told them so, but it was not enough for them. I felt hollow and miserable that I had ruined such a beautiful thing. I hung my head and let a few tears escape. The magic must've sensed my sincerity; the vine in my hand sprang to life and gently brushed the tears from my cheek and chin before moving back to its place on the wall.

I admit that the fear kept me safely away from the mist and therefore away from the wall, but in that moment I had a burning need to touch the bricks. As I approached, the dark fog subsided, granting me passage, and I nervously touched my two fingertips with a kind gentleness to the cold exposed brick. A quiet calmness spread over me as I dragged my fingers along the wall and led myself farther into the forest where I'd never ventured. I breathed deeply, suddenly very relaxed, although a small voice within me was pleading for me to go back. To turn around. It warned me that I was not safe. But I did not listen. I could not. I was entranced, and I let the urge to seek out the secrets of the wall take over my body.

The vines along the brick spread themselves and crept along the wall with me. It was as though they were following me, wondering what I was doing. The trees grew thicker around me, making it difficult to see where I was headed. But I maintained my slow pace, all the while trailing my fingers along the brick until I saw a break in the forest ahead. The autumn leaves crunched beneath my feet. I must've been walking for quite some time because the sky darkened and a chill blew through the air. I wrapped my arms around my bare shoulders, cursing myself for not dressing warmer. The brick wall ended just outside the forest as I'd hoped it would.

The dark green vines stayed on the brick and two small flowers bloomed just above my hand. I stared at the beautiful pink petals, trying to gather the strength to touch them and wondering if I should pluck the flowers.

After all, the magic made them just for me.

My fingertips gently touched the delicate petals. A sense of profound calm washed over me, and the stem fell to my hand of its own accord. I brought the bloom to my nose and filled my lungs with the sweet floral scent. A soft smile played at my lips, and I silently thanked the magic and placed the stem in my satchel.

I always thought the gate was sealed shut with magic. The men who'd lost their lives decades earlier were the ones who were able to climb the gate. At the time, it was unbreakable and sealed with a magical force. The tellers of the tale were convinced that the magic allowed those men to climb the gate in an attempt to lure them to the beast, because when the screams started and the men ran back to the gate, climbing it in an attempt to escape, the vines wove in between their hands and the iron rods, tying their bodies to the gate and forcing them to stay on the beast's side. The beast who they'd sought to kill. The magic held them there until the beast came for them.

Recalling the story did nothing to disrupt the easiness that ran through me. Even as I imagined the screams of the men as the beast's claws dug into their backs and his teeth clamped around their necks, I did not feel frightened. My fingers grazed the cold iron, and I stared at its beautiful and intricate detail. I let out a small sigh in admiration of its beauty, and I did not react when the creaking indicated that the gates were moving, granting me entrance. After all, it seemed so natural that they would part for me. I had no idea why I thought that, but I continued watching with bemusement.

I looked beyond the gate at the massive estate. The castle was much farther back on the land than I imagined it would be. It's also made of old red bricks, and for a moment I wondered if it would feel the same as the brick wall, or if maybe I'd be able to feel the magic on that brick since I failed to feel the magic on the wall. There was a large garden to the right and although I wasn't sure if it consisted of vegetables or flowers, I was certain that the trees just before it were apple trees.

At the realization my stomach growled. My father has struggled since my mother passed away. He does the best he can, but it's no secret that we aren't well off. We often go without much food. Especially late fall and winter when the gardens are barren. Knowing there were apples just beyond the gate was enough to move my shaking legs forward.

I'd only taken two steps beyond the gate when a cream splash of color caught my eye. It stood out in the darkness. It moved my concentration from the right side of the estate to the left. I cautiously approached, listening to the click of my ragged shoes falling against the cobblestone path.

I was quickly able to make out that the cream colored item was a shawl dangling from a wood-plank swing that hung from the bough above. It must be from a very old, tall tree that'd grown in the forest and reached over to the castle side of the wall. I picked up my pace to get to the garment. Seeing the protective piece of cloth made me suddenly aware of the goosebumps covering my arms and how I could just make out my warm breath in the chill of the night.

The soft cashmere fabric was thick, and I covetously brought it up around my arms and wrapped it so that it covered my front just up to the tip of my nose. My face instantly warmed. Although it was plain, I felt beautiful dressed in the luxurious fabric. Next to a few of my mother's old dresses that I'd never dreamed of wearing out of fear of ruining the lace, the shawl was one of the finest pieces of clothing I'd ever worn. I smiled into the cloth and silently thanked the magic for their generous gift, letting out an easy breath.

The wind blew and gently rocked the swing in front of me. Feeling cozy in my shawl and relaxed by the scent of the flower, I took a seat on the swing and began to rock gently back and forth. My fingers wrapped along the rope, rubbing back and forth against the rough material. As my body swayed, I closed my eyes and the only regret that I had was that I'd not given in to temptation and come sooner.

The crunch of a heavy body approaching behind me made me snap my eyes open in absolute terror. *The beast.* Before I could move, I felt his hands brush against my neck. I stilled in fear and held my breath. My fingers gripped the rope so tightly that my skin burned and my knuckles turned white.

His hands gathered my hair and pulled it from beneath the shawl, draping it over my shoulder. I felt the hairs on the back of my neck stand as he exposed them to the chilled air while he twisted my locks and began wrapping them around his wrist all the way to the nape of my neck, fisting the last bit and causing just a bit of pain that, for some reason, sent a spike of wanton heat straight to my core.

I felt his hot breath along my neck and heard him take a deep inhale. He was scenting me. And then he tasted me. His large hot tongue left a wet trail along my neck from my shoulder to the sensitive spot just below my ear. That languid movement caused my pussy to clench in desire and I felt the warm moisture build, preparing me for him. I couldn't contain the small gasp of lust that escaped me, and I leaned into him as he licked me again. My breasts rose and swelled in response to his masculine scent. I instantly wanted him licking my now wet pussy. I'd give anything to feel that hot sensation along my sensitive clit. Soft moans escaped me as I imagined how it would feel.

He took in another scent and the rumble of his low growl made me whimper in submission as the tingling heat built inside of me. His sharp teeth nipped at my neck, making me gasp as he pulled my fisted hair to the right, forcing me to expose more of my neck to him. I panted and closed my eyes, waiting for him to claim me and own my body like the beast he was.

His other large hand explored beneath the shawl and dipped between my legs. His thick fingers forcefully pushed past the waist of my skirt and panties, finally brushing along my damp center. Loud sobs of pleasure escaped my lips at his potent, powerful touch. My body ached for more. I pushed my hot pussy into his hand and spread my legs for him as much as the swing would allow.

He groaned a deep sound of approval and nipped my neck once again. My body responded to his with heated and primal desire. The slow circles he pushed against my clit brought me closer and closer to my release as I rocked against his touch. Leaning my head against his chiseled chest, my body began to shake as my orgasm advanced. I felt his lips brush against my ear as he fiercely growled, "Mine," and bit down hard on my shoulder, breaking the skin while his fingers expertly pinched my clit sending my legs into a hot convulsion as my orgasm took my body with force. I threw my head back against the solid wall of hard muscle and screamed out as the pleasure devoured my body.

As I came down from the overwhelming sensation, I noticed the warmth his body had sheltered me in was receding. I took a deep breath and gathered my courage to look behind me. I parted my lips in shock. No one was there. I immediately stood on weak legs and searched for the beast. I began to think that I'd gone crazy and imagined his hands on me until I reached up to where he'd bitten me. The pain was evidence enough, but when I pulled my hand back and I saw the blood, I knew then that there was no way I'd imagined it.

But where had he gone and why had he left me unharmed? Better than unharmed, apart from the bite on my shoulder, he'd only given me pleasure. My brows furrowed in confusion and then sadness. Tears pricked my eyes. I parted my lips to call out for him, but stopped myself as I realized how dark it was and how cold I'd become without his body enveloped around me to keep me warm.

I shuddered then wrapped my arms tightly around myself. Keeping my head down to shield my body from the wind, I walked quickly to where I'd come from. I was relieved to find the gates still parted and just inside there lay the other flower that had bloomed. Only it was now no longer pink, but a vibrant red. I gathered the delicate flower and brought it to my nose, letting the soft petal brush against my skin as I inhaled the sweet scent.

As I brought the stem down to place it in my satchel, I heard movement behind me. I turned quickly, mostly out of fear, only to once again find nothing. The fear quickly subsided and I felt a sense of loss and dejection. I frowned but I stopped myself from being overwhelmed with sadness. I made a promise to myself that I would come back. With one last look at the large estate, I wrapped the shawl tighter and walked away from the beast.

Only once I was beyond the fog and past the forest did the shock of what I'd done and the horror of what could've happened occur to me. It hit me with such a force that my body felt drained of blood as the coldness consumed me and I collapsed in a frenzy of shudders. I'd gone beyond the gate. The realization was terrifying. And he'd touched me. I screamed involuntarily and shook at the memory.

Again, I doubted myself since I'd not actually seen him. My hand traveled to the bite mark and brought back the evidence of blood for me to see yet again. I screamed in horror and lay crying alone just beside the dirt road for what seemed like hours.

I swore I would never return. I would not trust the magic and allow it to entrance me again. I would not risk being caught in the hands of the beast again.

But that was months ago, and I miss the magic. Not only that, but I dream of the beast. It's not a dream I'd admit to out loud, but it's a dream I'd like to see come true.

CHAPTER 2

THE PRINCE AND THE BEAST

The feminine shriek beyond the wall alerted me to the trespasser. I anticipated the vines bringing me my prisoner and I waited. And waited. The only thrill that brings life to the surface turned to annoyance as I waited longer than I ever have before. The beast in me huffed in frustration and clawed to come to the surface.

It wanted to maim and kill whoever dared threaten us. Whoever had the stupidity or the ego to step foot on our land.

As my fists clenched and a low growl settled in my chest, I was all too aware I had no choice but to desire the same.

The damn curse forced me to obey the will of the beast. Gritting my teeth, I held back the disdain, only because I knew I would only hear howls. I haven't heard my own voice in years.

"Only the beast will be shown." A low, menacing growl escaped my lips as I remembered that cruel enchantress and her hissed curse.

It's not the magic I held accountable for my anger, though. It's the people who turned their backs on me. Pacing, I snarled, unsure of whether the sound had come from me or the beast.

Patience, I demanded to myself. Patience would be rewarded. I stretched my arms over my head and cracked my back and then my neck. Waiting for prey was far better than waiting for the rose to die, I reminded myself, only to be met with protest from my lesser half.

The beast howled impatiently and I silently scolded him. We would have our chance to see who the magic has captured soon enough.

My gaze slipped to the wall, and I resisted the urge to scale it in an attempt to see what happened to my prey. The magic had no mercy. If there was a trespasser, I was sure to see them soon. The faint memory of the cry begged for my mercy. Compassion pulsed inside of me and it was a feeling I'd almost forgotten entirely. I would instill a little fear into the children if the magic had not already scared them off. But the adults, well...they knew what they were doing. I couldn't let that disrespect go unpunished.

The beast whined, fearing for its life. Even after all these years, he was still scarred by the memory. I shook my head. No one had come to try to destroy us in many years. It was most likely a thief that had come. Someone to pilfer the gold and silver that still resided in the castle. I've seen the village's lack of wealth, and the people slowly disintegrate as corruption bled into politics. Again I snarled. If only I was still ruling. The beast clawed at me once again, the sharp claws demanding attention as anger took over. I let the outrage pulse through my veins. Anger was such an easy emotion to be consumed with, and at this point, I enjoyed it.

Every few months, another pillager attempted to climb the wall. They had hopes that I was gone or dead or that they would get by me and ransack the castle. I smirked at their stupidity. Poverty and desperation will make a man do many foolish things. They should choose a different path, because I'm far from dead and even further from merciful. They'd risk their lives coming to steal from me. I may have had mercy on them if I had control. But I do not. And the beast is ruthless. To the beast, it is us or them. It is war.

I turned toward the front of the property as I heard the creaking of the gate. My brow furrowed in curiosity as my blood rushed in my ears.

The gates let no one in. So why did they part?

A heat slicked across the back of my neck as I took a hesitant and careful step to the side to disguise myself within the shadows. Hope rose in my chest for the first time in years. Had the sorceress returned to break the spell? I walked quickly but silently along the edge of the path to the gate, hiding in the mist.

I caught the intoxicating scent of a woman, and the smell aroused me in a way that I hadn't felt in years. It was quickly diminished by anger. Whoever she was, she was no sorceress and momentarily I was enraged that I wasted energy on hope.

This woman who trespassed had taken what little hope remained and crushed it with her presence. I clenched my fists and silently approached. A snarl rose within me, but my breath did not let it leave my lips as I caught sight of her.

A different feeling entirely took over.

Her hazel eyes shone bright and longingly toward the garden. My heart thumped as desire rose and I attempted to swallow. Her small hands wrapped along her shoulders as a chill swept by. The cold forced her skin to flush; the color rose from her chest to her cheeks. It took everything in me to hold back the primitive groan that the sight of her elicited.

Her long lashes fluttered and she released a faint gasp, parting her lush red lips. Her brunette hair, ruffled by the wind, made my fingers twitch and ache to run through her locks. My eyes traveled down her curves and lingered at her wide hips and narrow waist. Perfect for gripping. My mind played tricks on me, imagining her on her hands and knees gasping for breath with those swollen cherry lips. I would take hold of those hips and thrust into her easily and deeply. She had the body to take a punishing fuck.

My dick hardened at the thought, and I stifled my groan yet again. The beast roared his approval inside of me. With one step forward, I dared to move closer.

The last thing I desired was to startle her or alert her to my presence. I can't let her see me. *Thump.* A pang of fear gripped me, but only for a moment. The beast lifted its head in curiosity at the thought. I'd never cared before whether or not I was seen. It's not like I was ever going to let the trespassers leave and if they were children, they should certainly see the beast to tell the village he lived beyond the castle walls.

So why did I care about this girl? I palmed my dick in answer. I wanted her. I let out a low groan remembering the vision of me fucking her mercilessly on the ground right before me. I wanted her more than my next breath. But I knew I couldn't have her. The beast reared back and slammed through me, fighting for dominance at the thought that I wouldn't take her.

Her breasts rose as she breathed deep and glanced to her left. The small action caught the attention of the beast and we both focused on our prey. I followed her gaze. I was momentarily shocked. The magic offered her comfort. But why?

The sight of the shawl broke my desire for her, and I again questioned her presence. Why had the magic let her in? She walked quickly to the shawl and huddled beneath it, making her look even more fragile and delicate. Her lips released a pleasing sound that made my cock that much harder. I waited for her to head toward the castle. Or toward the garden. Did she plan on stealing food? That would be forgivable. The beast huffed in disagreement. For her, it would be forgivable. My chest rumbled as the beast agreed, thinking of ways her insolence could be used against her.

I eyed her curves as her body gently trembled beneath the shawl. I wouldn't mind taking payment from her body. I'd give her anything she wanted within these walls to have her begging me for her release. I wanted her submissive and obedient. I grinned wickedly, waiting for her to make her move.

A small smile played at her lips as she sat on the swing. Nestled in the shawl, she laid her head against the rope as her thumb ran up and down the natural fibers. My beast panted, wanting her to run her fingers through his fur. He rubbed up against me, urging me to move toward her. My feet obliged. My gaze transfixed on the beautiful woman who seemed to want nothing more than to enjoy herself. I longed to give her pleasure. The beast howled in agreement.

We would give her pleasure and then take ours in return. My muscles relaxed as I stepped forward as quietly as I could and gave way as the beast fought for control. It was a rarity that we ever wanted the same thing. I won't waste my energy fighting him on this. She trespassed and now she's ours. The magic kept her here for us. Content and fragile. The beast's steps were not as stealth-like as mine. But his speed made up for the noise. The second she heard us approaching, I was already on her.

Her gasp was riddled with fear and shock as my hands graced her neck. The beast wanted to feel her hair. And I pined to wrap it around my wrist to gain control of her.

I needed her weak for me. More than that, I wanted to make sure she would not see me.

As my hands gathered her hair, she went rigid beneath me. Her hands grasped the rope in a way that looked slightly painful. My dick throbbed at the thought. I would give her pleasure so excruciating she would beg for more. Testing that theory, I fisted the remaining hair at the base of her neck and tugged just enough to elicit a soft whimper. My breathing quickened and I grinned as she clenched her thighs tighter, knowing she was warming for me.

The beast scented her, breathing in deep, and smelled her desire. His need to taste her overwhelmed me and he ran his tongue from just below her ear to her shoulder. She gasped with lust at the feel of him on her and a spike of jealousy drove through me. She desired his touch.

The beast bucked against me and I allowed him to scent her again. Taking in the scent of her sweet arousal. I moaned in unison with his low growl, making my chest rumble with approval.

He nipped her neck and I smiled knowing that he would

have me take her. I pushed against him, needing to touch her. He allowed it, too concerned with her exposed neck, a submissive pose. He pulled her fisted hair to the right, forcing her to expose more of her neck to him. My dick hardened watching her submission to him. I needed to touch her, to reward her. My fingers slipped into the waist of her skirt, searching for her slit. I groaned deep in my chest at finding her hot and wet. She wanted this just as much as we did. There's no doubt that I would be buried deep inside her wanting pussy in only a few seconds. I circled her clit and watched as she writhed beneath me. As soon as she came undone, I promised myself I would take her just as roughly as I'd imagined. I groaned at the thought of her tight, hot pussy clenching around my throbbing dick. Soon.

Those soft moans brought me to my knees, but as her body shook with the rise of her orgasm, I saw her eyes open. Before I could even begin to worry that she would see me, I recognized the daze in her hazel eyes. She was entranced. My heart froze and fell flat.

The magic had spoiled her. She did not submit to me. She was victim to the magic.

With a disgusted swallow, I attempted to gain control of the beast. Stop! I would not allow this to continue knowing that she was under a spell. The magic made you weak, made you do things you would hate yourself for afterward.

I loathed the witch, but the magic was my enemy. My

heart pounded in agony, tortured and tormented. It brought her here to tease me, to prove to me what a beast I really am. I won't let the magic take her as it has taken me.

The beast growled, "Mine" and I pushed back in defiance, but he'd already clamped my teeth onto her shoulder breaking the skin while pinching her clit.

I saw what he wanted. He wanted her writhing beneath me as I fucked her to the ground. Holding her down by her nape with one hand while the other gripped her hips and forced her onto his dick over and over again. He wanted me to rut into her dripping cunt and make her scream in pleasure until she was limp and sated. All the while keeping his fangs pressed into her shoulder. Forcing her to submit to him. To me. To who I truly am. The beast.

But I couldn't let that happen. As much as the beast and my dick protested, I would loathe myself afterward. She was under the enchantment. I raged against the beast as he growled with satisfaction at the mark on her shoulder. His focus on his mark gave me the power to take over. I willed my body to turn from her and when it complied, I used all of my strength to run from her. I pumped my legs hard, fighting against the pull from the beast as he roared in anger at being taken away from her.

It's only when we could no longer see her that he fought me for dominance. His only motive was to fuck her with primal need. I'd taken him from her, and he beat against me with a desire to kill. I took his wrath. After all, he may want to kill me, but he cannot. Had that been possible, I would have ended us long ago.

Only the sounds of the gates closing parted us from our rage. My spirit, weak from the fight, submitted to the beast's will with the knowledge that she was gone. He whined in agony as we watched her take a hopeful glance in our direction before leaving with sadness clouding her eyes.

Two months of fantasizing. Two months of remembering. Two months of longing to relive that one small moment...

Alone in the castle, time tempts me to a craze.

I can still taste her on my tongue. The beast lets out a soft growl of approval at the memory. I wish I hadn't let her go. If only I'd been strong enough to overtake the beast. I could've kept her until the magic gave her a clear mind once again.

With a clear mind though, she wouldn't want us.

My fist strikes the table, splitting the wood in half. The crack echoes through the vast walls of the castle. There's no doubt she only allowed me to give her pleasure because she was not of sound mind.

The beast snarls in protest. If she'd caught sight of my appearance, she would have run. She would have fought.

My dick hardens at the thought of her fighting me. A deep

groan of desire leaves me, and my perversion threatens to get the best of me. Fuck. I want that fight willingly. I want her to know that I will take her when she pushes me. I want her to want to fight me so I'll fuck her ruthlessly.

I want it. I want her. I always get what I want.

My anger subsides as I realize I can offer her whatever she'd like. I may be a beast, but there are certain amenities I can offer. She can be available to me. Subservient and willing. I'll have to train her, but I can have her. The thought brings back my hope. I don't need the curse to be broken to have her. I simply need to find out what she desires most. I need to know what brought her here. The beast's chest rumbles in agreement, and he begs me to search her out and bring her back here for us.

It's been months since I've had her and I'm tired of fighting the beast. I need her just as much as he does. I will find her and lure her back here. I grin as I realize it will be easy to find her. After all, the beast has marked her and his magic pumps through her veins. The beast may have claimed her as his, but this time she's mine.

CHAPTER 3

THE PRINCE AND THE BEAST

In the two decades that I've been condemned inside these stone walls, I've stared out of this window to the point of being pathetic. The chill in the air is cold enough that my breath is creating a fog, destroying my view. I scowl as my palm wipes away the offending haze. I don't know why I waste my time bothering with it. With imagining what used to be and what could have been.

My fisted, calloused hand rests on top of the frame and I lean my forearms against the cold glass, finally resting my head and closing my eyes in an attempt to reclaim my memory. This is the only window in the tallest tower that has a view of the village.

It's been so long, I barely remember the paths in the village, and they may have possibly changed. To plan the best route to take, I need to remember as much as I possibly can. Although the dark mist that plagues my existence makes it difficult, I can, at times, see the properties in the distance. I've looked out with longing these past years when the loneliness has overridden the anger of betrayal. Wanting to venture past the woods and set foot on the land that used to be welcoming and eager for my presence.

Today, there is no use in looking. Not a damn thing is visible from the tower. Not that I would be able to see *her*. There's no way I could possibly discern the tiny moving specks of humanity from this distance. It doesn't matter; determination sets deep in my soul. I'll leave tonight, regardless, plan or no plan. I *must* have her tonight. My need to see her tempting curves, hear her panting, and feel her tremble in my arms again consumes my very being. I'm obsessed with the way her lips parted in ecstasy at my touch. I dream of the tender and soft moans that escaped those lush lips. But all of it is just a memory or a dream—nothing more.

My fist pounds against the frame in anger. The crack of the wood splintering beneath the blow fuels my rage. The rumble in my chest makes me aware that the beast is in agreement.

We must find her.

I'm determined to have her in my grasp. Luring my little

beauty back to the castle may be difficult. I'll have to hide in the shadows and mist to avoid being seen. My hope is to find her asleep and use the magic of the roses to lead her to the castle in her dreams.

The magic is never on my side, but it craves her too. It desires her here. It must help me.

Tonight I will venture out into the dark and find her. I'll let the beast take control of this hunt since his mark will easily lead him to her. A low growl rumbles in my chest and I narrow my eyes. *He* will have control.

I don't care for the lack of control, but it is the fastest way. There are only so many hours of darkness. I only hope his desire to have her is greater than his need for revenge against the village. I strum my fingers against the splintered frame, then let the fleshy tips run along the rough, cracked wood.

I'm not certain I'll be able to contain him if he decides to take advantage of his freedom. If he seeks out my former ally who betrayed us. After all, his attempt to kill me would have also killed the beast. A deep sorrow rocks through my body. It was the last time I spoke to another person. It's been years since the day that treachery destroyed the final remnants of good in me. The witch truly won that day. I no longer only looked like a beast; I became one.

Years have passed, *years* without hearing the voice of another being. I've questioned my sanity daily. Wondering if the words I think in my demented head even exist. If I'd even be able to communicate once this spell is broken. I'm only given reprieve when trespassers find themselves at the mercy of my grip. Claws digging into their flesh, spilling the warm blood onto the ground. I can smell their fear in memory.

Sometimes I'd slow my movements just to hear them plead with me for mercy. So I could hear the long lost sound of another. *No, stop, please, don't.* I'm familiar with those words. I've yet to keep anyone alive long enough to hear more than a few stumbled words from my prey. The beast doesn't wait. He doesn't care to hear their words like I do. I scoff at my inability to tame him, to keep him leashed. He's so overpowering when others are present that I can hardly control my movements, let alone the ability to speak. Only growls and snarls find their way past my lips. If ever I could chain the beast back long enough to hear more from those who trespass, it would most decidedly be a one-sided conversation.

When I open my eyes, my scowl deepens as I glare at the bit of village that's visible. I struggle to remember where I used to venture. Who it was that I used to seek out. A snarl rips from my chest. *Fuck them! Traitors! I protected them! I gave my life for them!* And they not only turned their backs on me, but they fought me. Led by my former confidant and only friend. Power hungry just like the witch. That fucking mistress of the dark. Wanting me for lust and power. A deep, low growl rumbles through me. The beast loathes her existence as well. Our hate is equal and in unison.

It's been that long since I've had a woman. I scoff at myself. I had more than plenty before the witch cursed me with her jealousy. I take quick strides across the hall toward the bedroom and find myself staring into a mirror. It's cracked in three large, jagged pieces, but it maintains its place on the wall. I run the tip of my finger along the fissure. In one piece I'm able to see myself, the prince I once was. The wavy, dark brown hair is long enough to spear my fingers through. My blue eyes travel the mirror to another piece and golden eyes stare back. The face of a twisted snarl revealing fangs too large for its mouth and fur in place of hair glares back at me. *The beast.*

Rage consumes me and the desire to pound my fist through the mirror overwhelms my body. I crack my neck on both sides in an attempt to dull the anger. It would be no use to let my emotions run free. The magic only let me damage the mirror once. All I'll be left with are bloodied knuckles and the vision of the beast in my head.

I'm surprised by my restraint today—it must be that my mind is preoccupied with the thought of her. Of finding her. Keeping her. I grin wickedly as my blood heats and my body tenses. I *will* be keeping my beauty.

There's only been one exception to the beast's fierce need to kill in all these years. I don't even know her name. Not that it matters. I will call her mine. My dick hardens as I envision her lips parted in ecstasy while my fingers played against her soft, pale flesh, spreading the moisture from her hot center to her throbbing clit. I release a low rumble that vibrates through me.

I'll feel her beneath me soon. My scowl slowly morphs into an asymmetrical grin. I'll have her on her knees. Her hazel eyes watering as they stare back at me while I fist her hair and push my length all the way down her throat. I grip my dick tight at the base and stroke up. Using the drips of precum, I lube the head and work firm strokes up and down. I spit on my dick but in my head I imagine demanding her to do it.

"Again!" She flinches at my rough command but immediately obeys, spitting on my cock as I stroke myself. I maintain a steady pace as I see myself slipping into her hot mouth. She moans at the taste. She loves taking my cock however I'll give it to her. She's learned to live for it. A low groan of wanting escapes my lips.

Leaning in to obey my silent command, her lips wrap tightly around the tip of my cock. Her tongue massages the underside of my length as I push my way deeper into her throat. Her cheeks hollow as she sucks me down. *Fucking gorgeous.* The sound and feel of her moaning around my cock are heaven.

"Hands behind your back." She obeys my command immediately. I grip the base of her skull, fisting her hair and ruthlessly fucking her face. I slam into the back of her throat, making her gag. She takes it all. Those hazel eyes stare up at me as I choke her with my cock as deep as she'll take me, but I give her no mercy. I pause only to pull my dick out of her hot mouth and slap it against her face, leaving behind moisture on her flushed cheeks. She gasps for air but quickly recovers. Her lips open in an attempt to get me back into her mouth. So greedy for my dick. Such a good little submissive. Again and again I slap her face with my dick each time she attempts to take the head into her mouth.

Fuck yes!

I grip her small, fragile neck and pull her delicate body up off her knees, making her whimper, before I slam her lips against mine and force my tongue inside to taste hers. Our teeth clash before I bite her lip, scraping my fang against the lush, tender flesh, breaking it and tasting her blood. She moans at the assault. I can smell her desire.

I easily toss her gorgeous body over the bench and on her stomach, positioning the pale flesh of her ass at the perfect height. *Slap!* She yelps at the blow. My hand stings and my dick hardens. I give her more of the same. *Slap!* I smack my palm against her skin and then grab a fistful of her reddened cheeks, loving the feel of it in my grasp. She writhes and moans as I spank her ass. I run my fingers down her cheek to cup her pussy. The tips of my fingers dip inside her heat. *Fuck!* She's hot and dripping from her yearning need. Enough. I need to be inside her. Fucking her. Giving her what both of us want.

I increase the speed of my own hand stroking my cock. The velvet on steel glides easily as I leak copious amounts of precum. I picture myself fisting those beautiful, reddened ass cheeks as I pound relentlessly into her welcoming warmth. Her hot sheath grips my cock as she gets closer and closer to her climax. *Come for me, my beauty.*

She mewls under me as I pound into her without mercy. The bench, bolted to the floor, absorbs the blows. I fuck into her harder and faster as her moans of pleasure increase in volume and fill my ears. *Love what I do to you. Crave this as much as I crave you.*

Desperate for her climax, her head thrashes against the bench, and she gasps for air between her screams. *I own her in this moment. She is mine. All she'll ever be is mine.* I fist her hair and pull her head back, making her back arch.

She's beautiful and utterly perfect. Her loving this is the sexiest thing I've ever seen. I move my hand to her neck and squeeze around her throat, never losing my pace. She whimpers at the assumed threat. The small move causes her pussy to clamp down on my dick. Instantly, I respond by picking up my pace, releasing her throat only to strum her clit.

"Come for me."

She screams and falls limp against the bench as her climax hits her with a force that jolts her body. I can't help but grin as I ride straight through her orgasm. I can bring her to this point of pleasure. I can give her ecstasy. I wrap her hair around my fist, like I did the first time, and apply a bruising hold on her hip with the other hand. She's had hers, now it's time for mine.

Her slender neck beckons the beast to nip at her, to sink his fangs into her delicate flesh. I never relent the steady pace of my strokes. Her strangled cries of pleasure get louder now that she can no longer bury her head in her arms. The edge of her next climax quickly approaches. With my left hand gripping her hip and my right fisting her hair, I piston into her as fast and hard as I can as I feel the tingle in my spine making me aware of my own impending orgasm. A cold sweat breaks out along my skin, and I welcome it as I breathe heavily. The sound of our flesh meeting as I rut into her with a primal need fuels the need for my own release. I feel myself tighten and I find my release with hers as she screams my name.

My name...

My name...

She screams my name.

I pulse and warm come spills in my hand as I let out a low, torturous groan. My body jerks with pleasure and I lean against the wall to steady myself. I take a moment to catch my breath. In the years I've been trapped here, I've never dreamed of pleasure like that. Not in years.

Next time it will be even better.

The next time I come, it will be inside her.

CHAPTER 4

ELLE

The tips of my fingers trace the raised edges of the scar on my shoulder. I stare in the mirror at the small red marks that are proof that the beast really touched me. More than touched me. With the faint smell of fresh bread filtering in the back room and the clash of pans fading in the background, I sigh deeply and close my eyes as I recall the aching feel of his hard chest against my back. His warm breath teasing my neck. The sharp sting as his fangs nip my tender flesh. His hands expertly playing my body against me. A shiver runs down my body as I remember the passion I felt. In an attempt to steady my quickened breath, I brace myself against the sink. In my dreams, I imagine it was the prince.

My eyes find the scar in the mirror. I know better though; a beast did this to me.

I should be dead. *Why didn't he kill me?* I wasn't myself when I crept past the gates and into the clutches of the beast. The trance took me there. The thought is terrifying. I couldn't resist the magic of the beast. The horror of that knowledge has kept me far from the edge of the village. My heart sinks and my blood runs cold. No one has gone to the castle, no one that's still alive to tell the tale. Everyone fears the magic and even more so the beast. And yet, I did so foolishly.

This dark secret consumes me. I haven't told a soul, and I don't intend to. But every night I lay awake replaying the event and having the horrific thought that in my sleep, I'll be entranced by the magic and walk back to the wall.

Chills flow down my arms. I not only ventured past the wall; I let him have me and I survived his embrace. I thrived at his touch. I've never before felt the touch of a man. Yet I blossomed under the hands of a beast. My thighs clench as my core heats at the recollection. What's worse is that I want to feel him *again*. I ache to feel his hands on my body. Gripping at my blouse, I pull the fabric back up in an attempt to cover the scar and turn back toward the storage room. The desire to seek out the beast is only just shy of my fear of him and what he's capable of. My life may seem pitiful to some, but I don't have a death wish.

I know what he's capable of doing. The bench groans as I

rest on the edge of it, recalling the lure all over again. When I was in school, two older boys were bragging about how they were going to go to the wall. How they weren't afraid of the beast. Instead of warning them not to go, the other kids insisted they were lying. They told the boys they'd need proof. The boys foolishly grinned and boasted that they would bring back evidence of their conquest. That was the last day anyone saw them.

My throat closes and I restrain myself from going back to that place of regret. I pull the stained apron over my lap and hold onto it as if it could change what happened. I've felt so guilty for not pleading with them to stay away. I was too shy and embarrassed. Too skeptical that there was a beast. Although the thought of him kept me far away and I thought, perhaps, that's why the adults had invented the idea of him. To keep us from going too far away. The other kids didn't seem to have the same fear of the wall that I did. I felt like a coward as the two boys bragged about their intent, so I kept my lips shut tight and swallowed the need to tell them it was too dangerous. But after that day, there was more than enough fear and guilt to keep anyone else from suggesting to ever go near the wall. Or daring to think the beast didn't exist.

A loud crash in the kitchen brings me back to reality. With a startling jolt, I jump and quickly cover the mark before tying my apron in place. The dreadful thoughts cling to me all the while. With one last reminder that I'm at work and have responsibilities, I brace myself for the long day ahead. After all, the dough won't knead itself.

Another loud bang and a hushed curse greet me as I open the backdoor. It creaks gently although I'm not sure the older woman heard me come in.

"Are you all right, Ara?" I peek my head around the corner and into the small kitchen, careful not to overstep. Ara is a petite blond woman with streaks of white throughout her locks and a natural beauty. She's the epitome of motherly strength, and that's exactly what she's been to me since my own mother passed. Her lips purse as she clutches her hand. She doesn't have to respond for me to know she's not all right. I wince as she places her hand in the bucket of cool water meant to rinse the knives.

"The oven bit me," she responds playfully. Her hands have several burn scars on them from years of baking and mishaps in the kitchen. She looks up at me with a little smile playing on her lips. It must not have gotten her too bad if she's in good humor.

"Do you need any help?" I make my way to my small area of flour on a cutting board to continue my work but find the dough already kneaded. It's resting in a bowl with a thin cloth laying gently across the top. I'm only slightly surprised; I wasn't gone long but Ara is one to step in if she feels anything is behind.

"Is there more?" I'm quick to ask.

With a shake of her head, a defeated sigh leaves me. "No worries, my dear." She dips her fingers in a cup of cold water before looking back at me. "Could you clean up the front though?"

"Of course," I answer and return her simper.

I'm grateful to have any income at all. Especially one at the bakery. Ara lets me take home the stale bread. It's rare that any goes unsold, but if it does, she allows me to bring it home.

There's a constant dusting of flour throughout the bakery. Cleaning up the front is a task that will take all day, but I'm more than happy to do it. I strive to earn my keep.

Turning on my heels, I head to the front of the shop, the bay windows letting in more light than what's offered in the kitchen. Back to real life where I'm just the baker's helper and the candlemaker's daughter.

After taking stock of what will need mending, I walk out the back door to the well. My flats are worn almost too thin, and every small pebble is felt under my feet. I pump water into a bucket on the ground beneath the spout. With the heavy bucket in one hand and a rag in the other, a sigh leaves me. It's been three days since I last wiped everything down and it's in dire need of cleaning already. There's a small dusting of flour on every surface. It will take me all day. All day of silence, left alone with nothing but a mindless task and thoughts that refuse to let me sleep.

If only I could tell someone. If only I could make the

thoughts of the beast stop.

Just as I raise my hand to remove a basket of biscuits from the top shelf behind the counter, the front door opens with a groan and the ding of the bell. I turn to greet our customer with a smile, but my smile nearly falls as I see Lord Crawe giving me a cocky grin as his eyes travel down my body. I swallow tightly at his obvious craving.

Although he's more than twice my age, Lord Crawe's rather attractive. I suppose I've always been attracted to older men though. Something about the hint of silver at the temples and small wrinkles that form around knowing eyes, it just calls to me so much more than a smooth and charming appearance. The light stubble lining his strong jaw adds to his masculine appeal. The women are always gossiping—it's really the only thing to do in this town—and they say Lord Crawe and the prince were the most handsome men in all the village in their youth. They looked so much alike, many would've sworn they were twins if they didn't know any better.

He may be classically handsome, but I would never return his flirtatious tone. His sexual depravity is well known, and I do my best to steer clear of him. So much so that the dread I felt only moments ago returns fiercely, demanding my heart to race. He's often taken advantage of many of his servants, letting them go once he's had his fill. Only a few weeks ago he offered me a position paying almost double what the bakery pays me. But I kindly declined. I do not wish to be alone with him and there was no mistaking that his intentions were for me to be just that.

From what I gather in the years of whispers, Lord Crawe was the king's regent and the prince's closest confidant. If anyone has information on the beast, it would be him. When the village first rose against the beast, Lord Crawe put up a valiant effort in the name of vengeance for the prince, but he failed to kill the beast. It's rumored the beast nearly ripped out the lord's throat with his massive fangs, but the arrival of the townspeople sent the beast running for the castle, escaping with near fatal injuries. My eyes stare at the faint scar on Lord Crawe's neck.

Or so the story goes...but with rumors and gossip and tales as old as the town itself, I'm not certain what is true, and I keep my curious thoughts to myself.

After he propositioned me, I was hoping to avoid this man, but in this moment a small part of me wants to engage in conversation with him. To question and pry...I want him to tell me about the beast. Anything that he knows and everything he's willing to confide.

With my throat tight and my fingers twiddling in the fabric of my apron, I purse my lips at the thought. Lord Crawe isn't a man that would do anything without something in return. And I'm unwilling to pay the price he demands of me. I keep my lips sealed tight as I make my way toward him, my footsteps padding against the wooden floor. I will find someone else to divulge the secrets of the beast and my enchantment with him.

"How are you, my lord?" I greet him with the tip of my head, steadying myself in front of the bucket and folding my hands in front of me.

"Elle," is all he offers me, his tone deep and masculine. A heat of embarrassment flows over my skin as I wait for more, but nothing comes.

I haven't told a soul what happened. I haven't dared to admit that I was foolish enough to venture into the woods. That I let the magic weave into my mind and limbs, taking me closer to the beast. I'm not even sure if they would believe me, even with his mark on my skin. It's unbelievable that I survived. And like I said, this town likes to gossip and I'm not one to seek out that kind of attention.

"What can I do for you today, Lord Crawe?" I ask as politely as I can, my voice slightly shaken. I'm still a bit resentful from the way our last encounter ended.

"Please, call me Gavin." I'd really rather not, but I don't want to be rude.

"What can I do for you, Gavin?" My cheeks blush involuntarily. I'm sure he's used to hearing those words from his servants, and the moment I realize that, I wish I could take them back. The handsome bastard has the nerve to widen his smile and lick his lips. Some women would swoon over the look he gives me; at this very moment it makes me want to run.

He's a predator in every sense of the word. And I'm his prey.

He leans across the table, too close for my comfort, and lays his hand palm upward, brushing my fingers. I inwardly cringe, but I force my body to stay still. "You would make a beautiful wife, Elle." My name lingers on his tongue and it doesn't feel right.

I pull my hand away and fiddle with my fingers behind my back. I can't meet his eyes, so instead I stare at the smooth hand still open on the table. *Wife?* I have far too much respect for myself than to be married to someone as debauched as Lord Crawe. I part my lips to speak and attempt to harden my features, but his words stop my protest before it begins.

"I'm sure your father would agree to my proposal. Would he not?" I meet his questioning gaze and falter. He is quite handsome and I would never have to worry financially, but it would not be love. And I hope when I marry, my husband would be faithful to me. I purse my lips in response. I will have to tell my father immediately that I'm not interested, that I cannot be wed to a man who treats women as he does. Surely if I tell him I don't want to be married to Lord Crawe, then he will respect my wishes. *Wouldn't he?*

I give him a tight smile and clasp my hands in front of me. "I thought you were interested in taking me on as a servant, Lord Crawe? My father didn't think highly of that proposition." In truth, I hadn't told my father of the interaction or offer. I was mortified and I knew my father would be upset by the proposal as well.

"I asked you to call me Gavin, Elle." He admonishes me with a cold tone and narrowed eyes while removing his hand. "I'll speak to your father to clear up that misunderstanding." His eyes linger on my breasts as he speaks. I just barely resist the urge to cover them. All the while my heart races as if it's trying to escape and my body begs me to move. To be anywhere other than in this room with him. I pray he doesn't speak with my father before I return home tonight. I need to make him fully aware that I don't want to be given to Lord Crawe. Fear pricks along my skin at the realization that he'll most likely see my father before me. I push the apprehension down and square my shoulders.

"What was the misunderstanding exactly?" I ask.

The sly grin appears on his face once again. "I realize you're far too beautiful to let slip through my fingers. I hope I didn't offend you with the job offer." He waves his hand in the air. "It was merely an attempt to get to know you better."

I raise my brows at his ridiculous response. I'm sure he wants to get to know some of me better, if his returning gaze to my breasts is any indication. I'm not certain what to say in response so I decide to simply ignore it. I place my splayed hand across my chest and clear my throat. When his eyes find mine, I give him a tight smile and ask, "Is there anything I can do for you today, *Gavin*?"

He smiles and nods. "Biscuits. A half dozen, if you'd be so

kind." His baby blue gaze rakes my body the entire time he speaks. With my teeth clenched together, I squash my need to huff and turn my back to him while I gather the biscuits in a freshly cleaned cloth.

"Anything else I can get you from the bakery?" I ask with my back still turned to him. I breathe in sharply and jump at the firm touch to the small of my back. My body goes rigid.

He lets out a low, rough chuckle at my response and leans down to whisper, "Not today, Elle. But soon." The hot breath at my neck isn't welcomed. Neither is the threat. I turn quickly and press my back against the wall, pushing the biscuits into his chest.

"Ara!" I call out, nearly breathless. "We need more biscuits!" My heart pounds in my chest, but my face is devoid of emotion. I won't let him see how frightened I am of him. I can't be his wife. I won't. He laughs at my efforts and takes the biscuits from my hands, brushing my fingers with his as he does.

"I'll speak with you soon." His eyes search mine, but I don't offer him a response. As Ara makes her way through the kitchen, he leaves two silvers on the table, turns, and leaves with purposeful strides. It's only when the bell chimes that I let out a breath I didn't even know I was holding. The kitchen door opens with a telltale creak and Ara observes the shelf, nearly full of baked goods still.

"Are you sure? Have we sold all two dozen already?" Ara

glances at the shelf above my head before shaking her head. "Are you holding these for someone?" She questions me while pointing to a basket full of biscuits, but I'm finding it difficult to respond. My heart feels like it's falling and uncertainly swarms me.

He wants me to be his wife.

He will ask my father and...I don't know what my father will agree to.

A chill flows down my body and my legs weaken. I will have no say. Women do not choose their husbands. I can't control my expression in front of Ara; I don't try to, either. A look of shock and then worry crosses her face. "Elle, dear, are you all right?"

At her concern, I shake my head. "I feel faint." I don't want to tell her about Lord Crawe. It's one thing for me to hint at my distaste for him, it's another to speak ill of a lord. "I think I need to go home."

"Of course, of course." Her voice is gentle as she pats my shoulders while her eyes linger on the silver and then dart to the door. Her lips purse and anger storms her eyes. As I said, she's the epitome of motherly strength, but she knows just as well as I do that there's nothing she can do if Lord Crawe can persuade my father.

CHAPTER 5

THE PRINCE AND THE BEAST

As I near the edge of the enchanted forest, the thump in my chest rages and adrenaline races through my veins. Every movement is slow and calculated, although the beast inside of me is barely contained. The fallen branches crunch beneath my heavy feet making me pause my advance.

It's dark enough that my cloaked body mostly blends in with the night, but I'm all too aware that the mist surrounding me would give away my identity if my presence is noticed. Even though the night is cold, heat covers every inch of me as I slowly make my way around the last few trees obstructing my view of the dirt road. My calloused hands brush along the rough bark as I quietly step beyond the enchanted woods. The first step since I took refuge in the castle. I still my body and close my eyes to heighten my hearing. There's a faint chirping of crickets that inhabit the creek and the splashing of water most likely from toads and fish coming to the surface. The night life surrounds me, but I concentrate toward the village in the distance. Tilting my head in an attempt to hear better, I faintly hear a dog bark but after a moment everything is silent. Not a thing to hear from the sleeping village. It's roughly two miles ahead and the path is speckled with light from fireplaces and candles in the windows of some homes. There are darkened buildings set before the cottages and I know those surround the market. They should be vacant, but even still, I will be careful.

I cannot fail. She is my reward and I've waited far too long as it is.

My blunt nails dig into my palm as I clench my hand to form a fist. A very large part of me craves vengeance. I crave the taste of Gavin's blood. He could've saved me but instead he condemned me. A snarl rips through my chest as the beast fights for command. My step back is heavy and reckless as I attempt to contain him. I regret my thoughts of revenge. Now is not the time to tempt the beast.

I hold him back and concentrate on the object of our conquest. Her curves, her soft moans. The beast paces within me. He's impatient for her touch as well. I relax my shoulders and calm myself by picturing her lips on mine. I'll let the beast take over to find her, my beauty, but I need to concentrate on the desire to have her in order to distract the beast and control him. He can't wander. His lust for blood would lead to a massacre. And I'm not certain we would survive it.

It doesn't escape me that I am risking my life to steal her away.

With a deep breath, I slacken my massive body, feeling the beast's desire to come forward. He brushes against my chest and I don't push back. I feel my lip curl and my eyes focus. He violently breathes in the air, taking in the scents that surround us although he only seeks out one. There's no way he could scent her from here. I push forward toward the village. The beast happily obliges as an asymmetrical grin pulls at my lips. I know this is dangerous, but the risk is worth the reward. My heart pumps loudly in my chest, not in fear but from a rush of adrenaline.

Tonight we will find our beauty.

We will take her back to castle.

She will be ours.

CHAPTER 6

THE PRINCE AND THE BEAST

It's a rare day I give up so much control. It's unsettling to say the least. The beast has us barreling with an unstoppable speed through the barren field with only our beauty in mind, and he's loud as fuck. Anger bristles with his recklessness, but I don't dare take over. He's far faster than I could ever be.

There are no shadows to hide in, no place to seek shelter. Only a large open field of dead, dried-up wheat that separates the dirt road and the village. The beast decided to sprint through as fast as he could, not giving a damn about the noise and not caring about my desire to be cautious. Gritting my teeth, I bite down the protest, eager to move as quickly as possible. Late into the night, the village sleeps, and we hunt down our sole desire.

He's fast and the black cloak aids in blending us into the dark night. The mist that surrounds us will give away our identity if we're seen. But the beast doesn't seem to give a single thought to what would transpire if we're seen. I pound my fist against him, gripping onto the fur I've loathed for years, urging the beast to go faster and to seek cover behind the buildings in the market as soon as possible. He snarls his protest, and I resist the urge to fight for control or to make even less of a disturbance.

The animal side of me, driven by primitive need, truly doesn't give a fuck. His desire to reach our beauty is the only thing he can focus on. The image of her, just as she was, is a steady focus for me as well. I'm desperate to get her in our grasp, but we can't risk being discovered. I don't hunger for bloodshed...I only hunger for her beneath me. Wanting and writhing for more.

Anxiousness takes over and my blood rushes in my ears. It's so damn loud I can hardly hear anything else. Adrenaline surges through my veins.

If a single soul sees me and tries to attack, or if they only scream, the beast will kill them without hesitation. He's practically salivating at the idea of conflict.

As my heart rages with every sharp pounding against the hard and unforgiving ground, I second-guess my decision. I gave him full control so he could lead us to my beauty. But now I'm worried that I've relented too much power. He's surrounded by those he considers enemies and he's more than willing to rip their throats out if challenged. One scream will lead to the next and the beast won't resist the temptation. It'll be a massacre until we're forced to retreat. It's a war we can't win and one I'm uninterested in pursuing.

If any conflict occurred, I could try to fight him back and force us to run away from the village, behind the wall and into the enchanted forest, but that would mean leaving her behind. A prick runs down my spine as I grit my teeth, vying for control, as the beast releases a snarl. I may not want a bloodbath, but I'm willing to risk it for my own selfish desire to have her. If I see former foes I want to destroy, my anger will only fuel the beast's rage, giving him more power to disregard my requests. I'd be a liar if I said I didn't want revenge as well. I'm not nearly as bloodthirsty as the beast though; it's my only redeeming quality at this point. I only want to kill a select few— those who deserve to be slowly slaughtered by the beast for betrayal of the upmost kind.

Shoving the memories down in the depths of what's left of me, the rage boils inside as we push through the field, ignoring the dim lights of the houses on the far right side of us. They're only candles in the windows. Narrowing our gaze, we push forward with one thought in mind.

My beauty. Mine. Mine to take and mark as I wish.

Now is not the time for my bloodlust. I can't afford to

entice the beast with retaliation. I need to focus only on the temptation that's led us to this endeavor. A warmth flows through my blood. *My beauty.* I concentrate on my plan and on her curves. The flowers in my inner pocket will keep her calm when I place them against her cheeks for her to inhale the intoxicating aroma. She'll dream of the enchanted forest, the magic that lured her to me, and *us*—our touch and her pleasure.

The beast lets out a low growl of approval at the image I conjure. His thoughts obsess with her as well, biting her neck and claiming her under the moonlight. I despise that I shared my first touch of her soft curves with him, but without his desire for her, I'd never be able to have her. When she wakes after dreaming of us, she may imagine she came back to the castle of her own accord. Who am I to correct her? The beast grins wickedly and chortles. He's in agreement with our plan. When we get her back to the castle we may be in disagreement, but for now, we'll work together to capture our beauty.

Mine to tease and fuck, and his to claim.

It feels as if an eternity of torment has passed, but finally, we break through the field and the beast stalks around the first building. My heart pounds in anticipation and suspense. There's no light inside, but I recognize the structure as the trader's shop from long ago. He takes in a large breath and focuses his eyes across the dirt path to a smaller building and jogs to it, making far too much commotion, then circling it.

Thank fuck it's nearly midnight and there's no one in sight. I focus on the structure and take in the smells with the beast. The bakery. Hmmm. Our little beauty is a baker?

The beast snarls and huffs. He scents her but she's not here. My body heats with fear of not finding her, but the beast is unconcerned. She is marked and the hunt will be easy if his careful pace and unbothered steps are anything to go by.

With two firmly planted steps toward the village, the beast snarls and growls, baring his fangs. A spike of adrenaline cuts into my body as the fear of being discovered overwhelms me. I push forward, trying to calm the beast. Trying to remind him of our desire for her, but then I realize what he smelled, what he sensed that I couldn't.

Crawe.

I can't help the anger that envelops my very being. He was here. With *her.* What the fuck is he doing with her?

She's mine!

The beast roars in possessive agreement. Images of the last time I saw him unwillingly flash before my eyes. Anger pulses through my blood. Rage threatens to consume my composure. The beast sees nothing but red. I stare back at the eyes of my former friend, bloodied from my fist pounding into his face. The rancid smell of his fear of death clings to my nostrils. His throat is exposed as he attempts to get out from under me.

No! With my teeth clenched, I shake my head of the

memory and force myself to stop this train of thought. The beast must be tamed. Now is not the time for retribution. That's not what we came for.

Our beauty.

I will the beast to go to her, but his hackles are raised, his primitive anger overwhelming everything else.

My eyes widen and fear spikes through me. Fear of losing her. I can't afford to push the beast back into hiding without claiming our beauty. Especially not now. Now that I know Crawe has been sniffing around her. *I will not lose her!* My fists clench at the thought of him touching her. Having his way with her. A snarl rips through my chest and I've no idea if it came from the beast or from me.

I urge the beast forward once again, warning him of the potential loss of our beauty. I only need him to find her and then I will force him to surrender to my will. My head shakes as he huffs and snorts. My heart races. I'm not sure if he's willing to give up his prey for her. Killing Crawe will only give short-lived satisfaction. I'll still be forced back to the castle. The spell will remain, and the village will still despise and fear me equally. I'll have my day of retribution, but it will come with time.

Just as the enchantment promised.

I will him to remember her panting desire, the heat of her core, the mark on her shoulder when he bit into her. A low rumble confirms his need to feel her writhing beneath him. I see his desire to claim her, relentlessly pounding into her wet heat from behind with his fangs piercing her skin. Surrendering to his dominance and moaning with desire. I stifle my groan and palm my hardening dick. Fuck, I want her like that as well. Not yet, I remind the beast. First we must get her to the castle.

He scents the air again and ambles toward our beauty's trail, but I discourage him. Persuading him to walk slowly into the shadows. With a low growl he agrees, and I cautiously let him lead us to her, past the market, through an empty field. For once the two of us are of a single mind. Since this curse bound me to this wretched being, there has never been a moment of harmony until now. A wicked smirk curves my lips up as my hand gentles on the cold brick of the building as we take cautious steps forward.

His heavy steps, made with an uncontained eagerness, are still far too loud for my liking, but we're hidden in the darkness and the village sleeps unsuspectingly. As we come along a farm with a few horses and sheep, I urge him to go around the carts and make our way to the back. He doesn't hesitate to ignore my plea.

I don't have the time to fight with him. I grit my teeth and watch as though I'm not moving along with him. As though we aren't one being. The beast is quick and as he darts past the fence, the horses startle but remain quiet and alert. They may have heard our presence, but we're long gone before they have reason to fear us. One disaster averted. My heartbeat calms just slightly.

The beast continues his path unaware or uncaring of the potential demise we just escaped. I'm surprised by his focus and his agile movements. I no longer want the beast to move slowly. We're in the center of the village, surrounded by homes. Any noise could wake the people. We need to get in and get out as quickly as possible. The adrenaline pumping through me is enough to make a lesser man shake. I thrive with it. Feeling the dangerous rush.

He picks up his speed as he scents the air again. His head bows and our eyes focus on a small cottage with a lit fireplace. We round the house quietly. He's found our beauty. Quiet sobs halt us in our tracks. As I still with recognition, the beast flinches with what seems like concern. Our beauty is hurt. Every muscle in me tightens and as he scents the air for the pungent smell of blood, but there's none. My brow furrows with his confusion. I push against him, in desperate need for control.

Crawe was with her and now she's injured or...harmed in some way.

Twigs snap under the weight of my step as we remove the distance from the woman who's become our obsession. Another quiet sob and my heartbeat slows as I close in on her.

Thoughts run wild in our mind as we near the dim light of the window.

She could be upset about a number of things. Hell, Crawe may have been at the bakery after she'd left. I'm most likely being irrational, but I cling to that thought. Her sorrow has nothing to do with our enemy, but she must be calmed and lured to sleep. The beast relents his need for dominance. He has no interest in being in control with her in this state. I feel his pressure against me, wanting me to calm her, subdue her. He wants her in a state of arousal and desire. Just as we come up to the old window of the cottage, and I dare to brave a look inside, a man's voice is heard. The beast's hackles raise. I steady him to wait and listen.

"Elle, please understand." *Elle.* Our beauty has a name. I whisper her name and let the soft sound linger on my lips. My blood heats with satisfaction.

"I can't, Father!" I close my eyes and tilt my head to hear better. *Can't what?* After a moment of nothing but her gasps for air between loud cries, she speaks again.

"Please, tell him you've changed your mind!"

"Elle, you know I can't do that." His reply is sorrowful.

Her defeated tone nearly whispers, "I can't marry him." My eyes widen and my fists clench. I calm myself and the beast, it's no matter. We're taking her tonight. She will not marry. She doesn't belong to anyone but me. The thought barely settles the beast. He paces inside of me. His need is crude: to feel her body against his and remind her of his claim.

As the conversation continues, I keep in mind that it is

irrelevant. She will be in my bed by morning. *Elle is mine.*

"Lord Crawe will make a good husband." His tone is placating and hopeful. I just barely repress the growl and the growing rage. I remind the beast; we'll have her tonight. *He will not touch her. She is ours.*

Elle attempts to speak, but nothing discernible is uttered. All the while, I stay in the darkness outside of the window, waiting for the moment her father leaves her alone.

"You'll have some time to get to know him." Her response to his placating tone is only a grief-stricken sob. "When you're my age you'll understand, Elle. He'll take care of you."

Some time passes with silence. I wait with bated breath. The beast pushes forward with impatience.

Quiet but steady steps, followed by the creak of a door closing, suggests her father has left her alone in the room. She continues to cry, although now her sobs are nearly silent and interrupted by shaking breaths. After a long moment of silence, I hesitate to look but the urge is too strong and I cave to temptation.

The dimly lit fire casts small shadows across the room. I quickly make out what looks to be a rather small bedroom. A cot in the corner catches my eye. I make out her small form huddled under a blanket. Her body shakes gently with her sobs.

My heart clenches in pain. Doubt plagues my conscience. For the first time in years I feel sympathy and compassion. It's paralyzing. Everything in my being warns me; I *need* to ease her pain. Her pain is mine, the thought comes from the beast. Surely it's only so she'll be more willing to stay with me. To do as I please. If I make her content then she will be in my debt. Hopefulness and delight replace those unwanted dreadful emotions. Since she's unhappy here, I can take advantage of her situation and use it to keep a hold on her. A wicked grin pulls at my lips as my plan takes form.

We'll wait for her to sleep. The beast nods in agreement.

Then we'll make our move.

CHAPTER 7

ELLE

I'm not aware at first, there's no tingle of distress or any alarm whatsoever. I drowsily yawn as I stretch my body, completely unaware. Although, I'm warmer than usual, more relaxed even. As though I've slept through a million pleasant dreams.

The first hint is one of surprise: the winter cold hasn't crept into my cot while I slept. A small smile plays on my lips as I sink deeper into comfort. I dreamed of his touch again, but this time it felt more *real*. My pulse quickens and the heat intensifies. His masculine pine scent is all I can smell, his low growl of desire is all I can hear, and the deep rumble of his chest against my back makes me feel nothing but lust. With my lips parted in desire and my mind lost in fantasy, I arch my neck and clench my thighs in the memory of his teeth nipping my flushed skin.

Instantly, I'm paralyzed, my body rigid. My eyes widen in shock, very much awake and aware that some realm of my dream is very much a reality. With a panicked racing heart, I'm as still as can be as the terror sweeps through me. His warm breath tickles down my neck and the moment I question whether it's him, there's a sting of a bite on my earlobe.

My heart races in my chest, so loudly I'm sure he can hear. I'm very much not in my own room. The wealth that surrounds me is not mine nor is this comfort.

The least of my problems is knowing there's a hot, massive, hard body—definitely a man— pressed against my back. And I'm no longer clothed. I gasp as I feel his hot, hard cock against my upper thigh. My breath hitches and my pulse scatters.

My body seizes in fear at the thought of what he may have done. Clenching my thighs, I don't feel different. The small movement makes him stir behind me and I struggle to remain calm.

Slowly, ever so slowly, I peer down my body with minimal movement and see the remnants of dried fluids smeared on my stomach and on the sheets. He marked me...with...his come.

It doesn't take more than a quick look around to know exactly who I'm with.

The beast.

It's nearly too much as my body trembles and a small part of me screams *I've done this*. I never stopped dreaming and fantasizing. I willed this to be. With a heavy inhale, his warmth plays at the back of my neck, sending goosebumps down my body.

It's a weak attempt, but I try to pull the down comforter that's wrapped around my hips up and over my body, but it doesn't budge.

Quickly, yet as calmly as I can, I turn away from the chiseled chest and wrap my arms around my body in a pathetic attempt to guard myself. A chill from the air replaces the warmth I've felt at my back with the movement. He doesn't attempt to pull me back and I wonder if he's asleep.

If there's a chance of escape.

With a concoction of emotions—fear, anxiousness, and hope—I take in my surroundings, my eyes darting quickly around the expansive room. Velvety thick curtains, such a dark red they're nearly black, line the window. A plush, deep-red rug with Parisian patterns lies on the stone floor. The walls are decorated with beautiful scenic paintings and a large old intricate mirror that's been cracked and tarnished with patina.

For a moment, I doubt my initial assumption. Glancing at the bed, his large foot is pressed deep into the mattress over the comforter, preventing me from shielding my body. My

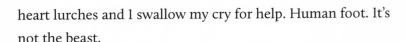

heart lurches and I swallow my cry for help. Human foot. It's not the beast.

Crawe.

My heart stills and a sob rocks my body. No. *No, no, no, no.*

An overwhelming sense of defeat and betrayal makes my heart slow and my blood run cold. He's taken me. The memory of yesterday hits me with a force that makes me bury my head in my arms and turn away from the hard body molded behind mine. My body trembles. *No!* How could Father let him take me?

Betrayal forces tears to prick my eyes, but they stop as a large hand wraps around my upper arm, rolling me back into his hard chest. As my body trembles, the rough hand moves over my stomach and brushes against my breasts.

My nipples harden at the gentle touch and my pussy clenches. I instantly recognize the feel of his skilled hands. *The beast.* Heaving in a breath, my mind is tormented.

I stare in the mirror, searching for any sign, but I can't see him. This isn't a home in a village, this is the castle. It must be. It's far too large.

Even still, I war with who it is behind me. Whose bed I'm in. Staring down at the hand, much larger than Crawe's, hairier as well. Far more masculine and hardened with work the former assumption would never do.

It is the beast behind me.

Did I come here from the spell? Did the magic lure me in my sleep?

All the questions bombard me as he splays his hand against my stomach, and I relax enough to give in to what he wants.

How the hell did this happen? And what have I done?

My heart beats wildly as his fingers run slowly down my skin, running small circles as he makes his way down past the curve of my hips. His hand moves to my inner thigh, and I instinctively clench my thighs together, preventing him from traveling any farther. I swallow thickly, uncertain how he'll react.

I'm naked in his bed and I don't know how or why. My blood rushes through my veins with fear. How can I escape? My eyes search for an exit but even if I found one, my body is frozen in his arms. A low warning growl breathes against my neck as his hand gently squeezes my thigh. His warm tongue licks my shoulder where he bit me, where his mark scarred my skin, and I find myself easing my thighs open for him. A sense of comfort washes over me.

Desire flourishes in the pit of my stomach as my neck arches, giving him access to his mark on me. It's like falling, like being back on the swing. My hand drifts to lay on top of his. Because that is where it's meant to be.

My body bows against his and his deep growl vibrates through me. As his licks turn to nips, my heartbeat picks up with excitement. Pure lust surges through my blood. His touch instantly eases every tense muscle in me and my mind is quick to follow, the racing thoughts blurred and muted until there is nothing but him.

I expose my neck to him in complete submission. A deep rumble in his chest vibrates against my back and heats my dampening core. A fire instantly sparks and a need to touch myself overwhelms me. My hand moves to find my release, but his hand captures mine and he nips my earlobe in admonishment.

"Mine."

CHAPTER 8

THE PRINCE AND THE BEAST

I'm in awe of the power the beast holds over our beauty, over Elle. The magic of his mark is undeniable. I didn't know how she'd react, but even in my wildest dreams I couldn't have imagined it'd be this easy. She's giving herself freely to him. The moment my lips brushed against the crook of her neck and the beast pressed against my chest, there was a shift. Her fear and worries just vanished as I licked his mark, giving in to his need to do so.

As a soft moan slips from her lips, I wonder how long her compliance will last. The beast and I take turns petting her body, although I maintain control of our form. His need to be present is too great for me to take over completely. And, if

I'm honest, I enjoy watching his power over her. She's not in a trance from magic. This is something...different. She's simply at ease. She *trusts* him. She really shouldn't. His intentions with her aren't moral. But how can I object when I desire the same?

He wars inside of me, desperate to take over, but I hold him back, gritting my teeth and pressing her back against my chest, my hand splayed over her stomach. She's mine. It may be his mark, he may have power over her and a pull I don't understand, but she is mine.

It killed me to not strip her down before we got her back to the castle, but the risk was too high to indulge. I waited until her breathing was deep and even before slipping in through the front door. Her window was far too small for my large build. With the beast eager but compliant, I quietly crept into her room and placed the flowers at her cheek. I wasn't sure how long I should wait so I gave myself a reprieve and watched her swollen breasts rise and fall. I observed a blush run slowly through her chest and up to her cheeks. Her plump red lips parted and she moaned softly. I knew she was dreaming of us, of our touch. With the magic and the pull of the beast, I stole away my beauty with ease.

My dick twitches with need, reminding me I was hard as fuck as I listened to those sweet sounds pouring from her lips as she slept. All I could imagine was pushing my length into her mouth. I want nothing more than to claim every inch of her, in every way my depraved mind can imagine.

As soon as we were within the walls of the castle and had her to ourselves on the bed, the beast became untamable. He obsessed over claiming her; his thoughts came back to the full moon and taking her under it. I've never understood the beast or the thoughts he puts in my mind. I swear at times I am crazed by his demands to shift, to run, to claim dominance.

He couldn't savor the moment as I was. Two decades I've been alone with my misery, confined to these walls without a soul and this beast inside of me, but now I have her. *We have her.* I need her to want my company as much as I want hers. I need her to live for the pleasure I can give her. I stroke myself again thinking about her wanting me—no, *needing* me.

The beast doesn't understand subtlety; he doesn't understand waiting. All he knows is that she is ours.

It was hard to resist giving in to her moans and pleas in her sleep. But I need her to be willing. I want her to truly enjoy the moment I bring her to pleasure time and time again. I want her to arch her back and present herself to me to take her however I'd like. A groan leaves me as she rocks against me slightly, my sweet beauty. I desire surrender from her like I have never felt before.

I lightly stroke her inner thigh and she parts her legs with ease. She moans softly while her head rests against my chest. The rumble of approval comes from the both of us. I crave her submission as much as he does. The beast continues to marvel at the scar on her neck while my eyes and hands roam her delectable body. Her soft pale skin begs to be marked. A wicked grin pulls at my lips. The beast agrees and I suckle her neck to rectify the situation.

I run my hand down her stomach, circling her belly button, then I continue down her body to run the tips of my fingers through the soft, trimmed hair on her pussy, watching for her reaction. Every movement is calculated; I'm careful to keep myself from her sight. She cannot see me or I might frighten her.

The need to observe how she responds to my touch is far too great as I run my fingers past her clit and down to her pussy lips, spreading them gently and dipping inside just enough to get her honey on them. Her eyes stay closed as she's in utter rapture from my touch. These stolen glances will be branded in my memory, I'm all too sure of it. Heat rises inside of me and my body aches for more.

I drag the moisture back up to her clit and rub circles against the swollen nub. Her head rolls back as she pants, and I can see her parted lips and her hooded eyes. *Fucking beautiful.* My chest swells with pride. She thrives with my touch. I lick my lips with the need to taste her, but I resist. Fear sweeps over me. She hasn't agreed to stay, and I won't let her see me until she does. I need to know she won't fight for me to keep her before I can bare myself to her. If she denies me, I'm not sure I will be able to contain the beast. Nor do I have any desire to. She is mine. She will submit; it's only a matter of what it will take to secure her obedience.

Tonight will be for her. I will give her unmatched pleasure until she's sated. Then I must give her space. I'll leave her to roam and see all that I have for her here.

The beast stirs in protest, and I hold him back. As my hand stills, fighting for control, our beauty stirs. It's only then that he's subdued, his focus on her pleasure.

The plan must work. I will please and sate her, allow her to take in all the castle and the magic can offer, and then she must agree. Only then can she see me.

I'll have to leave notes for her. That's the only way I can communicate. Anger swarms in my veins causing the beast to release her neck. Small bruises mark her delicate flesh. Depraved thoughts swarm my mind.

She is trusting of our touch, but how trusting? If I could get her on all fours, I could lap at her from behind without her seeing me. The beast growls in agreement, causing Elle to jump suddenly and her body stiffens.

The pounding of her heart makes it far too obvious that she's awake.

I gently stroke her clit again, and the beast nips her earlobe and down her now-marked neck to her shoulder. He laps at his mark, drawn to it with arrogance. He already sees her as his. But I need more. More than her submission in fear and in trust, I need her desire to please me. To be her reason to live. A darkness sweeps over me at the thoughts of what we could have together. *It is fate.* The thought whispers in the back of my mind and shivers run down my spine. *She is mine.*

With my hand gripping her hip, I nudge her forward, giving slight pressure. It's a gentle command and one I'm certain she'll understand. Her shoulders stiffen as she sucks in a breath. Adrenaline rushes into my veins. She's hesitant to move but she doesn't object, so I push a little harder. The bed groans and my cock leaks with precum as she complies, rolling onto her stomach. The small pants and shuddered breaths invigorate me in a way I've never felt before. Her lush curves tempt me to take her as she settles into the bed.

Resisting my own pleasure is difficult, but the thought of her cunt on my tongue is all I can focus on. Her scent makes my mouth water.

As I move to my knees, I spread her thighs wider while lifting her hips. A soft objection in the form of a murmur makes me pause. She pulls away slightly, so I release her, giving her time. Her breathing is heavier and I'm all too aware that fear lingers in the unknown.

I gently pet the small of her back and the beast licks her scar once again. She buries her head in the crook of her arm and shies away from the beast. A groan of disapproval leaves me, and she shudders. Far too much fear worries her. Regret comes over me; I should've tested her readiness before I put her in such a vulnerable position.

With a pounding in my chest, I hold back the beast and

sneer at myself.

Obviously she's vulnerable, naked in bed with me. But she didn't fear my touch. In this position I'm sure she's afraid I'm going to fuck her. It would be far too easy. She's no match for me. As much as that makes my dick hard, I desperately crave her surrender. I want her mewling with need, her face pressed into the sheets and her ass propped up for me to do as I please.

And I sure as fuck don't have her submission as she cowers under me.

The beast doesn't register the reality as I do. I can't have her scared of either of us...but she should be scared of the beast. His good temperament relies on her obeying him without question. He's unreasonable and an even greater monster than me. I covet the same as him, but I have patience where he does not. The years weigh heavy on me. I cannot lose her.

His hackles raise inside of me as she denies him what he wants. An anxiousness leaves a cold sweat rolling down my back, knowing his anger will only grow.

With my lips traveling slowly up her bare back, I lay myself beside her and pull her back against my chest. Back to where we were. In an attempt to not only soothe her, but to position my hand between her legs. My little beauty needs a release. She'll be more accepting of my dominance over her body once I've shown her that I'm capable of giving her pleasure and that her release is my priority. Her pleasure, her willingness. Fuck, it's all I've dreamed of since I first saw her.

With my fingertips trailing down the curve of her hip, I focus on the smell of her arousal. The beast relents his irritation and pursues nipping at her nape and down the back of her shoulder, reminding both himself and her of his claim. It causes a chill to run along her skin. Goosebumps spread down her skin all the way to her lush hips.

The image of lining her curves with gentle, open-mouthed kisses flashes in my mind, but I refrain from trying to pull the beast away from her. Not only would that anger him further, but she may see me if I ventured to kiss along her body.

It'll have to wait. I'll please her with my touch for now. Once I have her on all fours, I can worship her body and gain her submission. A grin pulls at my lips as I know I can then take her anyway I wish.

I take my time with her, playing with her and listening to all the feminine sounds that pour from her lips. Her chest rises and falls with each heavy breath as I toy with her. She writhes gently in my grasp, the flush in her cheeks letting me know she's getting close.

With the tips of two fingers, I dip into her heat and then bring them back out, putting feather-light pressure against her nub. She's tight and hot and it takes everything in me not to groan in the crook of her neck, throw her onto her stomach, and slam myself to the hilt inside of her. My beauty mewls and pushes her ass against my hard cock, her back arching gorgeously so.

Fuck yes.

She stiffens slightly at the realization that she's pressed along my length. There's a small gasp and then she rocks again, as if testing me. My chest shakes with a rough chuckle against her back and my warm breath trails down her neck. She shudders and her small breasts bounce just slightly when she does. The beast nuzzles into her neck in approval.

Her blush spreads over her chest and onto her cheeks. I don't relent my ministrations. As I dip my fingers along her folds, I have to suppress a groan; she's fucking soaking. She's so ready. I breathe into her neck while I put more pressure on her clit. I'll get her off this way and then she can come on my tongue. Only then will I push for more.

Her body trembles as I increase the speed and pressure. Her head thrashes from side to side but I lean my head against hers, stilling her against the pillow and preventing her from moving any farther.

"Take it." I'm not sure if the words are whispered by me or the beast. We're both thinking it. The need to have her find her release on my hand overwhelms my entire being.

I need to feel her quiver with pleasure. Her breathing becomes frantic pants, and her body lightly shakes as a sweat breaks out along her chest. *Yes!* Like the bastard I am, I pull my hand away just as she's ready to come. Her eyes spring open as I lean back and her mouth parts in protest. But there's no need. I'm dying for her release just as much as she is. I smack my hand hard against her clit over and over, and the sound of the slaps fills the room as her mouth screams a lost, silent plea. Her body jolts and spasms as her forceful orgasm pulses through her limbs.

I'm focused far too much on her expression. So much so that if she wanted to see me, she could with how reckless I've been. But her eyes stay shut and when she does open them, she doesn't dare look at me.

As she breathes heavily and desperately tries to steady her shaking limbs, I nudge her hips once again. She easily falls limp on her stomach, and I smile when I compare her willingness now to the last time I tried to get her into position. I lean down and kiss her ass cheek softly while stroking her back. Rewarding her for letting me pleasure her. After all, she is being a very good submissive.

I kneel between her legs and once again attempt to put her on all fours. I slip my fingers under her hips and wait with bated breath while she complies. She steadies herself on her knees, with her hips in the air but leaving her upper body against the mattress. I grin against her lush curves at her submission before kissing her cheek once again. All the while, I pet her lower back soothingly to keep her calm. I bend down lower and lap at her from her clit to her core and dip my tongue all the way in. Her first reaction is to buck forward from surprise. My grip on her hips keeps her from getting far, and she's brisk in efforts to get back into position for me.

For a moment I think she'll look back as I move behind her, my hand wrapping around her throat from behind and then up to her chin. I take my time, adjusting her head so she stares straight ahead, and when I take my hand away and she stays still, I kiss her once again.

The sight of her cunt is better than I've dreamed. With a languid lick, I reward her. Then my hands move from her hips to aid in pleasuring her.

She writhes under me at the touch to her sensitive clit. I'm not gentle in my touch, I'm fairly rough with her. I fuck her with my tongue but pull back when I feel an obstruction. Her hymen? Please, let it be so. Sitting up behind her on my heels, I cup her pussy with my hand. One hand is on her neck to keep her still, the other moves between her legs. Slowly, I push two thick fingers into her tight sheath. I'm not even knuckle deep when I feel it. My breath leaves me in a rush. A sudden desperation overwhelms me to be inside of her. To rip through her virginity and bring her a pleasure no one else has brought her before.

A moment passes as thoughts war in my mind. I debate on testing her willingness by rubbing the head of my dick against her entrance or continuing with my plan to taste her. Bringing my fingers to my lips, I taste her again and close my eyes as I savor her. She's so fucking sweet, a delectable beauty. As I enjoy her taste on my tongue, I lose control and madness consumes me.

CHAPTER 9

ELLE

I n an attempt to calm my racing heart, I breathe heavily into the mattress. My ass and inner thighs sting from the beast's coarse hair rubbing ruthlessly against me. He *used* my body. A heated wave rushes through me, tingling my limbs. I can still feel him behind me. His teeth rake down my neck, teasing me in ways I didn't know existed. He left me aching in longing for him to do what he must've wanted. I don't know what's wrong with me. The need to have him inside of me is overwhelming. *How could I want such a thing?*

I should be grateful he didn't do what he could have so easily done. He could have overpowered me, he could have forced himself inside of me. I don't even know him and yet I feel owned by him.

I've been taught to fear him, yet I crave his touch. With his large form hovering over my body and forcing me into the position he desires, mixed emotions fight within me. I want him to take me like the savage he is. Subconsciously, I bite down into my lower lip at the realization. He is gentle, yet rough. The heady mix fuels a fire inside of me.

Yet, at the same time I long for his merciless desire to claim me as his, I'm all too aware I need to flee from this imprisonment. I've not laid eyes on him and somehow he's made me his captive. As my chest rises and falls with slowly steadying breaths, fear trickles in.

With trembling limbs, I push off the mattress and quickly pull the heavy covers around me, finally able to shield myself although there's nothing to hide from. Without warning, he left me panting on the bed, not a word other than "Mine."

A chill runs through me and a false sense of security temps me. Questions race through my mind in an effort to dim whatever magic lingers. How will I get home? Will he even let me go? Mixed emotions run through me at the thought of being held captive.

Holding the fine linens against me, I take in every inch of the room, searching for his form—or anyone at all. There's not a soul with me. The floor creaks under my weight and that's the only sound except for my beating heart.

Swallowing thickly, I search for my clothes. They're

nowhere in sight. And what a sight this place is.

The room is nothing like my own. Carved and painted wooden furniture fills a massive room. I've only seen pictures and heard stories of wealth like this. Thick drapes that would surely keep the chill outside in the coldest of winters. Large glass mirrors that a dozen could see themselves in at once. I've only a small hand mirror from my mother. It's rare to come by.

My gaze darts to the door as I contemplate a step. Holding my breath, I take one, careful not to make a sound. I creep quietly to the armoire in the corner of the room. My fingers itch to open the drawer, to see what lies inside and perhaps find clothing. My breath hitches at the floor groaning when I shift my weight.

I slowly open the drawer and wince as it creaks. I hold my breath as my body stills and my eyes dart to the door. I don't know what he wants from me. The thought that he'd be unhappy with me sends a chill down my spine. I don't know how he would react.

I know one thing for certain in all of this: I do not want to anger the beast.

Above all else, I don't want to die.

As fear wraps itself around me, so does the magic. I can feel it, soft and caressing, but I'm all too aware it's attempting to deceive me, to keep me calm in a manner I should not be. I know nothing except that the beast has taken me.

After a moment of staring at the door, I swallow thickly, ridding myself of an ounce of numbing fear. If he heard me, he's unconcerned.

The heavy blanket slips slightly and as I pull it up, the floor creaks again. Staring at the door does nothing, there's not a sound at all to be heard.

Gathering up my courage, I pull the drawer out and gasp when I see its contents. Dozens of gorgeous blouses hang in front of me. I hesitantly reach out to feel the soft fabric between my hands. Smooth silks and soft cottons of all colors make up a simple yet beautiful wardrobe. My eyes catch a small note sitting on the right stack. I have to go on my tiptoes to reach it.

Wear the blue dress.

My body stills and my eyes fly to the door again. A chill sweeps down my shoulders and the magic follows it. It's such an odd sensation. The will of survival and my fear are at odds with a magic that wishes to soothe me under false pretense.

My shoulders rise and fall slowly. I know better than to disobey the beast.

In a wave, I feel heady. I remember his hands on my body. I remember the feel of his tongue along his mark. I'm vaguely aware the magic is surely toying with me. The memory is vivid and lures me into a contentedness and desire I've never felt before.

One I've only felt in my dreams of the beast.

I run my free hand along the luxurious fabric until my fingers linger on the pale blue dress. I pull the garment away and study its intricate detail. The cream bodice is laced up the front and the dress has a full flowing skirt. It's beautiful and certainly something I'd pick for myself if I could afford to have such nice things.

Tiptoeing across the floor, I place the dress on the bed and go back to the armoire. There are two small drawers at the bottom, and I pull them open in search of undergarments. I find a drawer of house slippers. The hides are stiff and definitely newly made. Unlike the paintings in the room and the furniture. Looking over my shoulder, I study the dress once again. It's new.

Did he buy these things for me? My mind whirls with questions and thoughts brought on by the unknown until the magic touches me again. This time from the tip of my nose, reminding me of the rose, and then lower to my lips, reminding me of him. It eases me to the point I nearly drop the blanket. Its movement is what brings me back to the present.

Without thinking much of it, I slide my feet into the slippers and sigh at their comfort. They fit me perfectly. Never have I worn such quality and comfort. I'm struck with the realization that everything in here is new.

My throat dries. He chose these for me. How long has he been planning this? The magic seems to drift away at the thought, leaving me alone with a chill that no cover could warm.

I try to remember how I got here, but I'm at a loss. I fell asleep crying over the fact that my father was willing to offer me to Crawe, even against my wishes. Betrayal shoots through me. It seems I'm only capable of being held against my will. It's only a matter of which beast has possession of me.

CHAPTER 10

THE PRINCE AND THE BEAST

That didn't go according to plan. I pace outside of our room, listening intently. I wish I knew what she was thinking and how she's feeling with everything that happened. I watch her small, delicate body move with grace as she explores our room. I finally have some use for the enchanted mirror the sorceress left me. I smirk wickedly; I wonder if she would've given it to me had she known this is what I'd be using it for.

I smile as I see her pull out the blue dress. Satisfaction settles deep in me, stirring the beast from his contented slumber. It's good that she listens to simple commands. My fingers rub against the scruff on my chin. I wonder how well she'll listen to the rest of my orders. The beast snickers as he sees my training plan for our little beauty. First, I'll get her settled and then I'll show her what I want from her.

I stare into the mirror, waiting for her to see the blindfold; I slipped it and the note under the door. I need it. I know the minute she looks at me and sees the hideous beast, she'll never agree to stay with me.

CHAPTER 11

ELLE

I know the peacefulness I feel is likely not my own, but I can't deny the sensation of warmth and luxury that surrounds me when I pick up the dress. There's a vague prick at the back of my mind that warns me not to fall into comfort, but it dulls with every passing second. The gown truly seems to have been made for me. The cloth is expensive and well-tailored so that there are no misshapen seams. I know it will feel even more luxurious against my bare skin.

For my skin is still bare. Every time I register the feeling of being completely exposed, the magic wraps around me again, making the shame of being naked in a place that's not my home easier to bear.

After all, he gave me a dress. It will all be all right so long as I wear it.

The note didn't have instructions to put on undergarments, nor are any laid out, so I pick up the blue dress from the bed. Swallowing thickly, I lift it over my head and let the fabric fall in a wave over me.

Covered, I feel no less exposed than before. Having such luxurious fabric directly against my skin makes my nerves sing. My nipples, already sensitive, peak at the slip of the silk. Nervously, I brace my hands on the bed and steady myself even as the magic comes to soothe me again. Will it always do so? I think, because I have lived near the forest so long, that it will. The magic has been a constant presence, though it is faint in the woods, for as long as I can remember. Although this feeling, in this moment, is stronger and nearly like a lullaby—not the nightmare I've been taught it gives.

If I stay here, for always, will I feel this peace for the rest of my life?

"Always" is frightening to think of, and the magic doesn't seem to want me to dwell on it. I find it much easier to concentrate on the slip of the silk over my hips and the way the air moves underneath it. The quality of the dress is as luscious as the house slippers on my feet.

A pricking sensation at the back of my neck warns me that I'm being watched.

But when I whirl around, my hands coming up to cover

my breasts even though I'm clothed in the blue dress, there's no one in the room. The mirror looks back at me impassively.

No one has come in to lay eyes on me. It only felt like the beast was watching. My heart beats faster as new fear is blanketed by a fresh wave of magic. The magic is always at the ready, waiting for me to act or react to the presence of the beast. It is a strange thing to be surrounded and calmed almost every minute, as if the magic knows the danger of the beast and understands that it cannot leave me alone in my mind for even a second.

Dizziness sways me for a moment and I murmur for it to let me breathe. "Please," I beg. This back and forth wars within me. There's a whisper in the back of my mind that it will be all right. If only I do as the beast requests. Again I look to the front of the room, finding no one and feeling as if I may be losing my mind.

As the emptiness of the room sinks in, my eyes drop to the floor by the closed door. It is dark in the room aside from a fire in the grate and moonlight through the window, but I can clearly see the floor.

It is not empty.

There is a folded note waiting for me along with a length of black cloth.

With my heart in my throat, I approach the door on trembling legs and bend to retrieve the cloth and the note. They were left for me by the beast. The magic wants me to think that this is only right. This place belongs to the beast, and he can leave me notes and instructions any time he desires.

I have to close my eyes at the sheer idea of his desires. A wave of pleasure plays tricks on me as I cautiously run my fingers over the gifts.

The black cloth is as silky as my dress although a bit thicker. I test it between my fingers. My fear now is that the magic will need to tend to me so much that I lose the ability to think for myself. I need to maintain control of what I can.

I breathe deeply and, with as little fear as possible, I read the note.

The instructions are as clear as the command to wear the blue dress. *Tie the black cloth over your eyes.* There is no room to question what the beast has asked of me. He has left me no room to hesitate.

I find a pocket hidden in the folds of the dress and tuck the note inside, thinking it would be better not to leave it lying out. I don't know why. I do not know who else might reside here. I only know that I don't want the beast's orders exposed to anyone else.

With shaking fingers I tie the blindfold over my eyes. As he requested.

The fabric is as soft as my dress, but it doesn't allow an ounce of light in. With the darkness, my heart hammers.. I can see nothing through the blindfold and move back a few steps from the door, careful and hesitant, though I am sure nothing has appeared behind me.

The door opens with an eerie creek and my knees nearly buckle. There it comes again, the wave of magic. I try to resist, internally pleading that I will behave, and with the promise of such, the pull it has on me wanes.

I strain to listen, but the hinges are well maintained and don't creak.

Soft footsteps enter and begin to circle me.

Inwardly, I struggle not to panic. *Please don't hurt me,* I beg silently. *Please.* The memory of the swing comes back. The feel of him. The bite. All of it surrounds me and to my surprise, I also plead with the magic, *please let it be the beast.*

The footsteps stop behind me, and it is quiet for so long that my heart begins to slow down, and I start to think that whoever is in my room may have already left. Not my room. *This room,* I correct myself.

I try to distract myself by picturing the fine furnishings of the room I woke in. They were beautiful enough to take my breath away, but now in the dark, my memory of them is indistinct.

I try harder to remember, but it's as difficult.

Just as I lift my hand from my skirts, thinking to remove the mask, there is a movement behind me.

I freeze.

There is no word from him. I want to beg him aloud not to hurt me, but I cannot make my throat form the words. It's far too dry and tight.

The floor creaks.

I take a step forward and find myself at the dresser. With nothing else to anchor me I can't stop myself from gripping the edge. My knees feel too weak to hold me.

"Please." My voice is barely a whisper. "Let me go."

"No." The answer comes from directly behind me and chills travel down my shoulders. He's so close that the warmth of his breath on my neck causes a stir of both fear and desire. Goosebumps erupt down my spine and my whole body trembles within the soft silk of the dress. The beast is firm in denying me my freedom.

I stay as still as could be as the floor creaks beneath me with the shift of his weight and steps.

Then there are hands, strong and broad, on my waist. My heart pounds with how close those hands are to my skin. My dress may be well made but it is only fabric, and the heat of his hands seep through almost as if I'm naked.

The hands feel large, but human. I swallow again. "Beast?"

"Yes," he answers. It's him. I know it's him. But this...this is different. Human hands mean he is not entirely a beast. If he was, there would be claws tearing through the fabric of my dress.

"Move," he orders. The heat of his command brushes the goosebumps at my nape.

I take one step forward, easily responding to his authority.

The magic around me makes it easy to obey him. A very small part of my mind tries to fear it, but the magic is as palpable as his hands on my waist. It helps me to obey. I tell myself it is keeping me safe. But isn't the magic what brought me here?

I have no choice but to walk blindly, trusting him to guide me safely. My heart thuds in anticipation of what might happen when I stop. I sense that we are passing through the doorway of the room and out into the hallway. I listen as hard as I can to each sound, trying to discern what I can about this place I'm now being held captive in.

I cannot tell much, other than that we are in a hallway. I do not have a way to tell how long it might go on. The floorboards are even underneath my feet. It's comfortable to walk in the house slippers, which provide a subtle cushion under my feet and allow me to keep my balance.

With my vision obscured, my awareness of my body is heightened with every step I take. I try to learn more about the beast's castle, but my attention is captured again and again by the heat of his hands and the cool slide of silk on my skin. The distraction and the mix of emotions make it impossible to know where we're going.

I do not know where he is taking me. I have not had time to understand this place, and my breath comes faster as we move farther and farther away from the bedroom.

I tentatively raise a hand in front of me so I will not run into a wall or anything else. Blindfolded, I haven't been able to see how the beast's home outside that room is decorated. Is there art on the walls? Statues on stands?

Is it destroyed from his anger and rage like the lore has sworn for as long as I can remember?

He does not make me put my hand back down, though his hands flex at my waist. The softest sound emits from the back of his throat. A shiver moves through me as it meets my ears. It is not a threatening growl. I think it may be a thoughtful noise, but I cannot be sure.

The magic continues to surround me as we move, steadying my breath and taking the fear from my thoughts. Despite the magic, my mind still questions.

Where are we going within this castle?

Why do his hands feel so human when I know he is the beast?

What will he do with me?

Heat flushes over my body as I recall the possessive way he touched me last. He wrung feelings and sensations from my body that overwhelmed the parts of me that had remained innocent. Is the memory so vivid because it just happened, or because of the magic? Does the magic want me to think of him?

What is real and what is fantasy are often intertwined in one's mind. At this moment, I cannot tell the difference.

His hands flex at my waist once again. His touch confirms that these are the hands that touched me. Thick fingers that pressed inside me, searching until they found a barrier that hasn't yet been broken. A wide thumb rubbed my clit. He stroked my folds and tested how slick I was between my legs.

In my haze of fear and heady, forbidden desire, I heard what he said.

Take it.

Those hands also soothed the small of my back and stilled underneath my body. They are hands with the full capability to hurt me, I have no doubt, but he used them to pleasure me.

And to use me for his own pleasure, although he did not break through the last boundary of my body.

Is that what we are walking toward now? Is that what he has planned for me? Is there some other space more fitting for the beast to take my innocence than the bed? The bed where he already put me on my hands and knees, growled, nipped, and kissed me until I was consumed with the need I had for him?

I can't guess how this will go. The stories of my childhood swirl through my head. The beast and the prince blend together. The tale is both true and false, more innocent than it seemed and more dangerous, and I do not know how my story will end.

My breath becomes shallow, but this time the magic does not soothe me. It stokes the fire of my emotions, making the memories of his touch even stronger. They're matched to the heat of those hands on my hips, guiding and commanding me just as he did in bed. I am clothed, for now, but under the influence of the magic, my desire for him grows. It would be better if he was simply touching my skin instead of the fabric.

Is it the magic that plays these tricks? Or is it simply the dreams I've manifested for myself?

The confusion I feel between what I know to be right and the base urges of my body tightens, making it difficult to breathe.

My outstretched hand meets something made from wood. The curves underneath my fingertips make me think it is a door frame. It's more intricate than any door frame I might have seen in my former life. My father did not have the money to spare on decorating his home. Not when we were struggling to eat after my mother passed.

I know it is only an object, but the way the curves feel in contrast to the beast's hands make my breath catch and I stop.

The beast's front hits my back. Instantly, I'm hot all over.

His chest is broad and strong, like his hands. I expect that he will pull himself away from me to put distance between us again, but he shifts slightly and presses himself closer. His hands tug gently at my waist. There's more physical heat from his chest, and it seems to surround me at the same time the magic does.

I need him. I need him to be inside me. There is no reason for him to wait to have what he wants, and I know he wants my innocence because I feel his attraction, too. His heart beats steadily against my back as I arch, making contact at more places. Every breath I take is warmer than the one before. *How could I want such a thing?* This time, the thought is a mere whisper, and I know that is not because of the magic itself. It is because the feel of his body is overwhelmingly tempting.

Every instinct in me craves to have me turn around and put my face in his neck. To inhale his scent. What would he do if I left a trail of kisses up his neck? Would his flesh respond to me the way I'm responding to him? I do not have the bravery to attempt it, but something in me wonders if I need bravery at all. Turning around would be disobedient, as he has only told me to walk and hasn't commanded me to face him, but the heat between us is a sure sign that he wouldn't reject me.

If I tilted my hips just so, I could press my body over his cock. I do not, but not because I fear what he might do.

I fear the magnitude of this wanting and what it may turn me into. Would I still be myself if I succumbed to the passion I feel for him? It cannot be a passion that I would be allowed in any other circumstance. I could never feel such passion for Lord Crawe. I cannot bring myself to tolerate the man, much less want him, and yet here with the beast, my body is alive with the forbidden possibilities he offers.

For the first time since we left the room, I do not care about the blindfold. It does not prevent me from feeling his body touching mine, and I can sense his strength and feel it without being able to see. It does not prevent me from wanting him and from feeling a slick heat between my legs.

It does not prevent me from wishing to stay here and take no more steps until I have had more of him.

Again, my mind whispers the question that came to me after he left my bed.

How could I want such a thing?

I do not know. I only know that I want it, though I could not say what it is exactly I am so feverish for. My mind offers many possibilities, and each one is as forbidden as the last. They are things no innocent woman would dream of asking for or having, and certainly not from her captor, from the beast.

"Please," I whisper, my voice heady as my plea slips from between my lips.

I do not know what it is that I am asking the beast for. I can only hope he gives it to me.

CHAPTER 12

THE PRINCE AND THE BEAST

Elle's body pressed so close to mine is fucking heaven. I've never felt such a stir of desire and pull. Not a damn thing in this world has brought this feeling over me. She is the only thing I can smell, feel, think about. *Fuck*! What does this woman do to me? Is it her? Or is it what I've become? My obsession with every small breath of hers is undeniable.

I breathe in the scent of her hair and her skin and the warm heat of her. She's already aroused, her lithe body arching tentatively against mine, and I'm drawn to the scent of her sweetness, too. More than anything else.

I'm almost overwhelmed by the delicacy of her scent and how quickly it has changed in my home. I distinctly remember the scent of her skin outside as I carried her through the enchanted forest. Elle was not as warm in her bed as she could have been, and I wrapped her in my cloak to protect her from the chill of the night, but it seeped in next to her skin.

The night air had been fresh and had the ever-present scent of the magic behind the enchantments. Elle's face and hair had been slightly cold when I arrived back home with her, but she warmed quickly when I brought her to the bedroom. Her scent has warmed and grown more complex from only one night with me. The beast is far too aware, and I urge him away. The only thing more surprising than my obsession with her is how the beast listens now that we both have her in our grasps.

Yet the trappings of her old life linger under that new scent. There is the bakery where she worked, handling sweet things and breathing in air that was warmed with the aroma of rising dough. There is the faint tinge of her fear, not of me but of the man that her father might have given her to.

The beast stirs but does not growl and leap to the forefront, an odd reaction when the memory of her father's words is so vivid in my mind.

These are the beast's senses, not mine, although I do not remember now what it was like to be without his enhancements to my human senses. So many times over the years we have battled for dominance, the beast taking control and making it clear I could not defeat him, or me shoving him aside through only the greatest effort. There have been times when I wished to be free of him, unraveling our separate ways of being so that I knew where he ended and I began.

If Elle didn't smell so sweet, I might be angry at the closeness of the two of us. It wasn't always this way, for it can't have been, but with my nose pressed to her hair I am accepting of the beast's embedded nature within me. I still know his presence as a curse, but I cannot help enjoying the benefit. There is so much purity, yet intense longing, in Elle's scent. The sweet-salt scent of her arousal blends in equal measure with yesterday's breeze in her hair and the bed sheets we slept in and even the way I put my mouth and fingers to her skin and made her come.

I breathe her in again.

Then again.

I realize I'm cautious because I expect the beast to lunge forward, seizing control and having his way with her. He abandons himself to his urges without understanding the human world. He only wants what he wants. I take such deep breaths because the opportunity is rare when I am in full control and not at the mercy of the beast's animal desires. I want to remember this about her every time I am the one at the forefront. Every time I have control over my hands and my body.

Not all of my body, however. There are some things I can't control even when the beast is sated.

And the beast is sated inside me. I inhale Elle again,

almost trying to tempt him, but he is restful. He does not try to push me away so he can follow his urges. This is a shocking proposition given how wild he was to claim her and have her. He could barely be controlled in those moments when his blood ran hot and the world turned red. He was considerably more animal when Elle's father spoke of giving her away to another man.

Now, he relishes her closeness and seems sure of it, though there is the idea within him that we should drag her to the baths and wash off all the evidence that Elle was ever somewhere else, sleeping under someone else's roof.

I expect the beast to rise at that thought, too, since he has been with me all these years, fighting for space and dominance, but he does not. That could be because he is satisfied with having her here. We are both satisfied with having her here.

But I am more satisfied, I think.

We have battled so many times that when he does not fight, uneasiness fills me. I try to sense more about him, but it is difficult to separate us with Elle so near. It is as if he has laid his senses over mine and they have melded together.

Again, I wait to see if the beast will try to wrest control from me, but he does not.

Elle's heartbeat slows down, but when I focus, I can tell that it is my own perception of time. It's almost as if it's stretching out so I can dwell on the feeling of her so close to me. We are at a threshold, the two of us. She has found the doorway to the staircase with her hand and hesitates as if staying here with me will get her what she wants.

What do you want, my beauty? I would give her everything for her to stay just like this. Allowing me to have her as I wish, obeying my commands. And giving me peace that I have not had since the curse was laid upon me.

Even with Elle's small frame in my grasp, the beast does not take over. I begin to relax into the idea that he will not, at least for the time being. He will allow my hands the freedom to explore her without the surge of animal lust.

Because of this, the lust I feel is entirely human. It is not altogether different from the way the beast wants and takes. There is an element to it that reminds me of the beast at his most dangerous, but I do not want to dwell on those thoughts when the way Elle said *please* echoes in the air around us.

My cock grows harder with her body against mine. For a few seconds I consider what it might be like to let the madness take me again.

She takes a shuddering breath, adjusting her body minutely. Such a small change, but Elle feels entirely new against me. It must be the beast's senses that allow me to see her movements with such clarity. It was the smallest shift of her shoulders and her hips, the most subtle repositioning, and yet it has also changed how the blood runs through her veins and how she fills her lungs with air.

I want to breathe with her. I want our two bodies to be connected by more than possession. I want them to be connected in every possible way.

"Please," Elle whispers again. Her hands remain at her sides, forearms over where I am holding her hips. It is far too much to bear without letting the beast claim her, but again, he does not.

Why is this happening? Is it because I want her in the same way the beast does? Am I cursed to want her so ferally, so dangerously, for all time? If that is the outcome of the curse, then it has done its job. If it has made me and the beast one and the same, there may be no way to divide the two of us.

I know there is no imminent danger that she will escape. The magic soothes her enough that she is more curious than frightened. Still, I'm torn between the old ways of wooing a woman with gifts and gentle words and the beast's way of claiming her. It is true that I stole her from her bed and brought her, sleeping, to the castle. It is true that she asked me to let her go and I refused. It is true that there is little pretty words will do when she knows she is not free to leave.

But there must be some balance. The more I breathe her scent, the more clearly I understand that the beast's urges are more similar to my own than I want to admit. I wanted to think I was fighting a monster, an animal, for control of my body, and that still remains true.

There are parts of me that are more beast than man.

And yet I will never know how I might have responded to Elle without this curse. Would the man I was before have walked through the enchanted forest and waited outside her window to carry her away? Would he have sought out the bakery where she sold goods and offered her a position in the castle or even suggested marriage?

There is no sense in thinking how things might have gone, because the curse is within me and has been for so long that I despair of ever getting it out.

But I do think of it. I do think of all the many ways I might have found her and wooed her and perhaps even spirited her away. And what I find when I let my mind linger on them is a very similar ending to this one.

It may be that I was always the sort of man who would take a woman this way.

I push that thought out of my mind. With the beast under control, I'm too eager to soak in Elle's presence at this moment, which has grown longer in spite of how time ticks endlessly on. Every year has seemed like a century since I was cursed, and for the first time since that day, I do not mind the way this pause in the hallway seems to stretch out.

I want to slide one hand from her hip to the front of her body, but I force myself to wait until I'm sure I am steady and the beast is quiet before I inch my hand forward to the front of her hip. She is delicate here, too, and sensitive. She gasps, her gorgeous lips part, but she does not object.

An unsolicited groan escapes me, and I do not know if it came from the beast or me as my cock hardens, wanting and needing more of her. *Of those sweet gasps.*

I allow myself another inch, my fingertips meeting the softness of her belly over the hard line of her hips. Elle takes shallow breaths, her pulse racing underneath her skin. I can hear her heart beating as well, as loudly as if it were in my own body. I can hear her dress moving over her body as my hand changes the way the fabric hangs. I can even hear the way her feet meet the floor, not quite steady, but not quite unsteady either.

I do not trust myself to speak. I have determined that Elle must see the castle and agree to stay before she can see me, and to speak aloud would expose more of me than she is possibly ready to witness. I cannot risk going against my plan, though I want to murmur words into her ear. I want to give her an answer to her plea.

I move my hand another few inches until my entire palm is against her belly. The muscles flutter as she breathes, waiting.

As I am waiting.

Though I do not know what I am waiting for. I am no longer waiting for the beast to lay his claim to Elle. I am waiting to know my own mind, but there is little to know when the urges of my body are so strong.

I crave her madly. It is in an animal way. I want to take her to the floor and push her dress up around her waist and have her quench both our thirsts, the beast and mine. I want to be buried inside her. I want to give her as much pleasure as her body can handle and help her to the ground.

If I stand here another moment, that is the course I will take and nothing will be able to stop me once I've started.

Before Elle can move again, I pull back, creating space between us, and lift her into my arms. It is an entirely different experience from carrying her while she was sleeping.

Elle's hands lift as though to remove the blindfold. I gather her tighter in my arms in a silent command to stop.

Breathing fast, Elle freezes then lowers her hands.

What would I see if she had gone against my implicit orders and removed the blindfold? How would her eyes look? Would they be filled with fear or would they be dark with the desire I can scent all over her skin?

I think it would be desire, and it pulls me to her almost unbearably.

I do not lower my mouth to hers or walk her back toward the bedroom. I do not put her on the floor to have her here. I master my own body first, ignoring the surging need in my cock, and move through the threshold.

The tips of Elle's slippered toes brush against the doorframe as we go, and then we are descending, Elle still and pliant in my arms. She does not fight me and does not seem to have any mind to. That could be her desire, or it could be the magic, or it could be both. I make no judgment. It is not the time to make a judgment. It is only time to move before the beast takes control again.

She stays that way, her scent filling my every breath, as I carry her downstairs to execute my plan without deviation.

CHAPTER 13

ELLE

The feel of the beast's body against mine is a heady one. Being held in his arms is no less so, and I feel a wave of what is almost like dizziness but more powerful as he walks down the stairs. Lust blinds me. Not the blindfold. Without my vision, I take note of every sound and every feeling. The strength of his arms around my body is like nothing I have ever felt...

Save for once.

The beast is muscled in a corded way I would only expect from a fearsome animal, but he has the shape of a man. I suppose this is what happens when a prince is sacrificed to a beast.

And it is almost as if the form of a man has been perfected in the beast's body. I wonder if this was done by the magic of the curse and the sacrifice as well. There is so much magic all around that I cave to it. The magic always extended beyond the wall, but in this place there is far more of it, and it is far more palpable. It's gentle yet intoxicating, much like the beast.

There are some parts of it that I cannot seem to shake off, although I do not want to. Being surrounded by magic is better than being surrounded by fear. I will accept the fine furnishings and the feeling of safety even if it is coupled with an intense desire that I am not sure is entirely my own.

We reach the bottom of the stairs. The sound of the beast's footsteps change on the floor. Heavier, more foreboding even. We must now be in a larger hallway or a longer space. I try to listen harder, but my attention is divided between the solid, warm sensation of his body against mine and the sound of his footsteps. They mingle together in my mind until neither one is clear and both are hidden by the beat of his heart.

I do not know.

He turns, his hips shifting subtly under mine and his footsteps making a new sound on the floor. The air shifts once again. Whatever room we're in must be very large.

Then he bends to lower me to the floor, and instinctively I grip his muscular arms and then catch myself, releasing my hold on him and grateful he does not respond. My heart beats faster, and I swallow thickly at the change in position.

He holds me by the waist until I am balanced on the comfortable slippers once more. I still under his touch, understanding that he does not want me to remove the blindfold. It follows that he probably does not want me to move beyond his reach until he gives me some sign or command.

The beast held me gently on the way downstairs, and he does not touch me roughly now. His fingers trace a path up my spine to the nape of my neck and linger there for a few moments. Goosebumps gather in the wake of his touch. Once again, I'm trapped with the constant thoughts of lust.

To my surprise, he works at the tie of the blindfold, loosening it until it falls away from my eyes. The silky cloth drapes over my shoulder and hangs there for a few moments until I understand that he wants me to take it.

I do, twisting it between my hands. He could use it to tie me, I suppose, but he hasn't done so yet. Adrenaline rages inside of me. My breathing comes in short gasps.

His hands move to the sides of my face with a similar gentle pressure. The lightest press at my cheeks tells me that I am not to turn around, so I don't.

I only realize that I have kept my eyes closed all this time when his footsteps retreat, growing quieter as he moves to another part of the room.

Then there is a silence that lasts for several beats. My breathing is loud in this quiet space, but when I allow it to quiet, I can hear another sound. It is impossible for me to identify what it is without opening my eyes. As I am still in the darkness behind my shut eyes, I'm still attuned to his presence. He has not gone far, and a few moments of listening tells me he is somewhere behind me, his breathing only slightly labored by our long moments of closeness upstairs.

When it's quiet for far too long, I dare to open my eyes.

It takes a few blinks to adjust to the moonlight streaming in through large windows along one wall. I can see fairly well in that light, although the ballroom is lit by fires in large grates across from the windows.

Awe overwhelms me.

I have not seen windows this tall or fireplaces this wide in any other building, and I marvel at the pearly light mixing with the firelight. It's a large room and a grand one at that. Intricate paintings and gold spirals decorate the vaulted ceilings, though I will need more light to see all of their details. I imagine lying on my back on the ballroom floor in the afternoon light, staring at the paintings for hours until I'd memorized every inch of them. They're beautiful.

The large windows are not only impressive because of the amount of glass it takes to make panes of this size, they are also beautifully framed. Everything in the room is elegantly decorated with the kind of expensive moldings my father would never be able to afford. A raised stage extends into the opposite wall, the empty space looking as though it could hold an entire orchestra.

All at once the ballroom seems even larger because of its emptiness. A ballroom of this size could hold dozens of couples. Stories of royalty and what once was in this castle come to my mind. I can almost hear the music soaring off the ceiling. I can almost see women in fine dresses and men in well-made suits twirling around me. Even with twenty couples I would still be able to put my arms out to the sides without touching them.

I drink in the sight of the room, once again taken aback by the amount of wealth signified by such a ballroom. Even in the dark, it's obvious everything in this space has a sheen, like gold and riches. It is different from the comforting furnishings of the bedroom I slept in, more dedicated to hosting and not a private part of the beast's home. Ballrooms are meant to be seen and danced in by guests, and this one is certainly meant to be seen. Each intricate detail offers another place for my gaze to catch and rest for a moment.

Moonlight gleams on the polished floor, which looks to be miles of finely carved hardwood. My feet tingle in my house slippers. I have never danced in a room so large, and I would do it now if I had a partner.

I have only dreamed of such things. Fantasies that I'd hoped one day would come true when I was a little girl. Love and happiness is found in these spaces. Although in this moment, the room is dark, cold, and empty.

With a prick at the back of my neck, I'm brought back to the present and drift from the dreams of a young and naive version of myself.

I consider turning to search out the beast with my eyes, but he has moved away. It is obvious he doesn't want me to see him, so I do not look, though I want to know what it's like to be spun around the most beautiful ballroom I've ever seen, even by moonlight. It would be even more breathtaking at sunset or sunrise when the light was warm and ample.

It is the most meticulously clean ballroom, too. Nothing like what I've been told, and it dawns on me that perhaps what I think I know is false.

I lower my eyes from the ceiling. It is not a loud sound but a soft one, swishing and swishing.

There. A broom sweeps the floor in the far corner of the ballroom, moving back and forth in a column of moonlight coming in through one of the tall windows. Broom might be the wrong term. I take a few steps, drawn by the movement. The sound is so quiet that it can only be a duster. It's not the sturdy sort of broom I use to sweep the bakery, one that would scratch polished floors like this. Shock holds me still with wide eyes.

The duster is moving by itself.

It is moving by *itself.*

Disbelief wars with my own vision and I have to touch it. To feel that it is real.

Before I know it, I am nearly to the duster, staring down at it, moving my head at different angles, trying to see if there's a person sweeping the floor. I do not know how they would remain concealed like this, with me staring at them directly, but when I stretch my hand out above the duster, I touch only empty air.

Cautiously, I lower my fingertips to the handle of the duster. Can this be real? Can this really be a duster sweeping by itself?

At the first touch, the duster falls to the floor with a loud clatter.

I whirl around, forgetting that the beast wanted to stay out of sight. "Is it real?" I ask, my voice echoing in the empty ballroom. Amid all the curling decorations, I cannot see him. After a few seconds I find the shape of him in a deep shadow on the other side of the room. A bit of the moonlight catches his eyes. That's all of him I can see.

The silence drags on. Perhaps he will not answer me. Perhaps he will write me a note and slide it across the ballroom floor. Suddenly I feel desperate to hear his voice.

"Yes," he answers, his deep voice sliding smoothly over the walls and floors. His shadow does not change. I can't see sharp teeth. I can't see his mouth moving at all. Only the vaguest outline. A darker shadow within a shadow.

With my attention back on him, my questions about the duster don't seem important anymore. Being able to see the man—the beast—who's keeping me here is much more urgent.

"Can I see you?" I ask.

"No." His answer comes much more quickly and definitively this time.

I don't know where the courage comes from. Perhaps my disappointment, perhaps my hope, although my father used to tell me the two are related. "Why not?"

There is another short silence that gives me goosebumps. There is energy between us, even separated as we are by the expanse of the ballroom floor. I listen hard for any hint of a growl or the beast readying himself to leap out of the shadows, but none come.

"Questions I do not wish to answer will be given silence. Is that understood?"

I blink away the shock of his answer. I cannot deny that there is sadness in his tone, although it is hidden by the regal command. That sadness is what makes me want to ask more questions. If the story about the prince who traded himself for the safety of the village is true, has he come to regret it? Or was that not what happened at all? What lies have I been told?

"Answer me," he commands.

"Yes." I breathe, accepting his terms.

Facing him makes my heart pound, so I turn and walk about the room, feeling as though it's alive. When I walk toward the feather duster it leaps up and begins sweeping again. When I move toward one of the windows, one of its lower panes opens and a fresh breeze blows in to cool my face. The moment I think I have had enough of the wind in my face, the window closes. Refreshed by the cool air, I turn to face the shadow where the beast is nearly hidden. His eyes shine in the moonlight, disappearing whenever he blinks.

"Is there anyone else here?" I ask cautiously. Though I do not speak loudly or shout, I can sense that the ballroom is carrying my voice to him so I will be easily heard.

"No."

My heart twists. "You're all alone?"

"Yes."

"Are you the beast?" I know he is. There can be no mistaking it.

But the beast does not answer. The silence goes on long enough that I know it is purposeful. He is choosing not to answer this question.

My heart squeezes in my chest and I can't deny the fear that lingers. "Are you who I was with...before?" I dare to ask.

"Yes." His answer is breathy, quickly soothing the bout of fear.

I'm careful with my string of thoughts and questions. Eager for answers. Eager for more. "Do the people...the townsmen...when they refer to a beast here at the castle, is it you they speak of?"

"Yes."

If this beast was living here, he may not be what the

townspeople said. He would not answer when I asked him if he *was* the beast. The people in the village refer to him that way, but...

Is he *not* a beast? Surely he must be. He is the one who bit me and marked me and brought me here in the night. There is no one else he could be.

"Put the blindfold back on."

I am so deep in thought that his voice startles me. I edge toward the wall, seeking any safety I can find, and press my back against it. The fear and desire and anticipation are only soothed a little by the magic. "Why?" I dare to question.

He moves in the shadows. "I want to feed you."

CHAPTER 14

THE PRINCE AND THE BEAST

I watch from the shadows as Elle lifts her chin then unwinds the blindfold from her hand. The moonlight lends her an ethereal beauty. She looks to be made from shadow and moonlight, the blindfold dark on her fair skin. Like this was all meant to happen in time and the moon became what it is just to exist for this moment.

She takes a tentative step away from the wall and lifts the blindfold to her eyes, wrapping it carefully around her head and knotting it in the back, her fingers nimble and her movements precise so that she does not tangle her hair in the knot. Elle slides her fingertips over the fabric, settling it into place. Her position near the window allows me to see every breath she takes. Shallow but not fearful. The scent of her is rich with nervousness for a few moments until the magic wraps around her again, quelling her fears.

I know she enjoyed seeing the ballroom. I heard her breath catch several times over as she discovered the moldings, the painted ceiling, and the glinting gold details that are everywhere in this room designed to awe and impress guests that come to the castle.

She loves the finer things. The art especially. It's curious how she responded to the will of the castle and the magic that holds power over nearly everything. Bringing to life her desires. I've never seen it work for anyone else. It's only ever bowed to my desires. And now...hers.

Elle is the first guest in a long time to appreciate the beauty of my ballroom. She stands tall and brave with her shoulders back and her chin lifted. I would not know by her posture that she was blindfolded at all, she carries herself so proudly.

Her posture falters slightly as she breathes deep, her shoulders begin to round, but she straightens again. The faint scent of dinner pulls me from my thoughts.

She will not go hungry when she is within these walls. She will not go without pleasure or warmth. I can provide for her what no one else can. Luxury and protection. Surely that will be enough.

I approach her slowly, keeping my footsteps even and

confident. The beast still slumbers inside me. It is only a matter of time before he wakes, reasserting his dominance, but for now I am in command as I cross the ballroom floor to Elle. Her breathing quickens as I get closer, but she controls herself, though she cannot stop her trembling completely. If I was not making an effort I might be trembling as well. That is how strong the pull between us is. That is how strong my desire for her is.

I take her by the hand the way I learned long ago, appropriate for escorting a lady across the floor. Her hand curls neatly into mine, though it is clear that Elle was not born into royalty. That does not matter to me. What matters to me is the heat between our palms and the brush of our fingers together. The soft silkiness of her skin affects me even more now that I have stood apart from her for several minutes. Every twitch of her fingers sends small shock waves through my being.

I need to bend my mouth to her neck to inhale her scent, but I sense that she would turn, putting her body against mine the way she did in the hall, and I might be lost to that sensation until the sun rose.

The beast stirs slightly, as if scenting the opportunity to claim her again, but he does not pursue it.

Elle walks when I put the slightest pressure on her hand, this time moving to my side instead of in front of me. She guides her footsteps so that her body is closer than it might have been, and we go out of the ballroom together.

My dining room is down a stretch of hallway. Elle's footsteps are soft but not tentative as she moves, her slippers almost silent on the floor. Every breath I take is sweetened by her scent. I have to summon as much control as I can not to push her against the wall and guide my hand between her legs. I think, from the way Elle's heart pounds and the rhythm of her breath, that she would melt underneath my touch.

Not yet. I will feed her first. Once I've satisfied her, surely, my offer will not be denied. Regardless of who I am. The fears scream in the back of my head, and I nearly cry out for silence. The crazed thoughts leave as quickly as they came as the magic surrounds us. Thankfully, Elle does not see my snarl. She is protected from every sordid thought I have.

The dining room I escort Elle to is a private one, though the table can seat twelve. Serving dishes cover the surface. Elle inhales the aroma of the food and lets out a small sound of anticipation. That sweet sound makes my cock twitch and yet again, I restrain myself. I guide her to the seat that will be at my right hand and take my own seat at the head of the table.

With a wave of my hand the covers of the dishes rise and float back into the kitchen through a door that holds itself open for them. Elle sits up straight, her hands in her lap, and I move my chair so I can more easily reach her.

Then it is time to keep my promise.

I pinch the finest morsel of meat, a slow roast of beef, between my fingers. "Open your mouth," I tell her.

She does.

The table is laden with a spread that would rival a royal dinner, including roasted potatoes and seasoned vegetables grown in the garden, and I feed Elle small pieces of them, her tongue sliding over my fingers. She chews and swallows and opens her mouth obediently for more. The magic allows for everything thought, every wish to come true, and so when water fills the pitcher and pours itself into her glass, I offer it to her. A smirk plays at my lips as she thanks me. As if I knew. As if I'm her hero.

Time passes easily and I watch her intently. With every bite she takes, my eyes flick from the scar on her neck to her lush lips. I'm obsessed with her satisfaction. Before long, the plate of sweets, chocolate desserts and pastries, and fruits rattles slightly and I move onto it.

I'm feeding her a piece of sweetened fruit when she closes her lips around my fingers and moans.

It is all I can do not to curse aloud. My cock strains in the front of my breeches. Elle's chest heaves as if the fruit has reminded her of more forbidden things she wants, and her arousal lingers in the air along with the food.

I draw my fingers out of her mouth slowly.

"Your kitchen has sent the best tonight," Elle remarks faintly, one hand curled around the edge of the table. She sits upright again, but she does not have her breathing under control. The tension is thick between us.

It's so thick that I cannot keep the words I wish to say inside. I cannot wait for the next opportunity to write a note. I keep my control over the beast steady, though it does not seem I will be able to divide my efforts for long if Elle takes this much pleasure in the rest of her food. Her lips glisten with the juices from the fruit, and I want to devour her. From her lips down her neck, lower and lower until I can feast between her legs.

"I will care for you if you care for me," I say, keeping my voice low to disguise the lust I feel. It is too blunt a proposal, but it's all I can do to contain myself. I know she will understand that I am offering her something of value. She has fed on a fine meal. She has rested in the most comfortable bed. She has seen the grandeur of the ballroom and knows by now that the rest of the castle contains similar riches.

Elle brings her bottom lip in, her teeth catching it for just a moment, and I am bowled over by a feeling of selfishness. It is selfish, the offer I am making her. No amount of food or beds or riches will equal what I am getting. I fight the inner critique of my selfishness down. We are already on this path. She will be mine and only mine. Always to stay within the castle walls and to forever submit to me.

Elle swallows thickly and asks, "For how long?"

For always, I bite down the response and offer instead a

truth more palpable. "For as long as I wish." That is even more blunt than the first, but equally true. There is little point in disguising the true nature of the terms from her. If she is to accept this willingly, she must know what she is agreeing to.

Elle hesitates, her mouth turning down. "My father…"

"Will mourn your loss, as fathers do." I am matter-of-fact, for there is nothing else to be. Fathers lose their children. That is what happens to all of them. "He will live and be unharmed."

Elle could not be more beautiful in the firelight. Even as she straightens, a frown mars her beauty for only a moment before she seems to come up with a negotiation.

"What if I wish to leave?" she asks, her voice not much louder than the crackle of the fire in the grate.

This is the part of the bargain that she will not like. I would keep it from her if I could, but I cannot.

"Then I cannot promise your father would remain unharmed."

She bites into her lip with more force, her breath quickening, and sits back in her chair, increasing the distance between us. Her fear is obvious in the air, and this time the magic cannot entirely subdue it. I would not have expected her to care so deeply about her father, who would have given her to Crawe, but perhaps I should have.

I lay my hand over hers where it is curled around the edge of the table. Elle flexes her hand, turning it upright so our palms are together.

"I do not wish to hurt anyone," I admit and the heaviness of it hits me unexpectedly. It is difficult to lay myself bare this way, although I am hidden from her by the blindfold. "I only crave you. It may pass, but I…" The words catch in my throat. "I crave you to the point of madness. So you will remain inside the castle walls."

Elle takes a shuddering breath. The beast notices this even from his resting state. Is it him who drives me to madness for Elle, or is it me? I have fought him for so long, but looking at her like this, obedient and compliant and hungry for me, makes me question whether I was fighting the cursed beast or my own impulses.

"No one has ever said such a thing to me before," she replies softly. I can hear her heart pounding in her chest. I think I may hear it even if I did not have the beast within me, for that is how much I crave her.

It is not enough only to hear the sound. It defies reason that no one has wanted Elle this much before, but then it is impossible for anyone else to need her as I do.

Unable to stop myself, I grip her hand tighter, as if unwilling to let her go.

Elle startles slightly at the touch, but after a beat she holds my hand back. Her heart is pounding harder than I realized. I can feel the life coursing through her, and the heat and warmth she possesses.

Elle feels so very human under my touch. So very alive and untouched by the wickedness of any curse. The way her heart beats is only for me, and I am entranced by it. I had expected more fear from her when she heard what I am offering, but it is small compared to her desire.

Her other hand lifts from mine as if to touch me, hesitantly moving toward my face.

I make a sharp *tsk* sound, drawing the hand that held hers back and warning her away.

Elle's hand falls to the table. Her hand curls around the edge once again. She worries at her bottom lip with her teeth, thinking.

"Is this..." Elle begins tentatively. "Is all of this an act of the magic?"

"I do not know." When I was first living with the beast inside me, struggling to regain control over my life, hoping that I might be able to leave the castle and live among people again, I had convinced myself that every raw urge was the fault of the magic and the curse alone. Now, having tasted Elle and felt the sweet clench of her pleasure, I cannot be sure. She is the first and only who has caused such madness.

Elle opens her mouth as if to speak but hesitates. I can see the smallest movements of her tongue in her mouth, rising to touch her teeth, and I want to hold her chin in my hand and keep her still so I can continue to watch until the sun rises.

And perhaps until the sun sets again.

Perhaps if Elle was here with me always, it would not matter how many days had passed. Until I saw her on that swing and knew her to be mine, the passing of time was slow and painful, as the beast dictated so much of my life and would not allow me to return to anything that could be considered normal. I saw the years stretch before me, empty and devoid of affection or even conversation.

"What is it you're thinking?" I question in her silence.

She takes a small breath, her heart slowing slightly underneath my palm.

"I am drawn to you as well," Elle admits in a soft voice. I could already feel the desire emanating from her, but it is a unique pleasure to hear her say something that should be utterly forbidden. She should not be drawn to me, rather repulsed, and yet...it may be because she has not seen me. She must agree. And then she will learn to live with the beast as I have. "If you allow me to send my father a note that I am well and perhaps a package of food—"

"No."

Her face falls.

"No one can know you are here," I continue. This is of the utmost importance. The news cannot spread in town that Elle is in my castle and intending to stay. I cannot have what happened before. She is my secret. And so she must remain hidden.

"I would not...I do not need to disclose my location," she

says quickly, her heart fluttering nervously in her chest. "Only that I am well and cared for."

Her voice shakes with the last bit and my mind reels with a compromise. If only to get her to agree.

Her intentions when it comes to her father are pure and more than the man deserves. Elle's father had her sleeping in a room that chilled her at night and did not value her enough to keep her away from men like Crawe. And yet she does not want him to worry after her. She wants her father to be fed, too. We're seated at a table covered in the finest delicacies my kitchens could prepare, and Elle is still thinking of her father.

"I will consider your request if you obey me and agree."

Elle exhales unsteadily. More heat fills the magic around her and between the two of us. The beast stretches inside me, beginning to wake. The scent in the air is undeniably one of lust, and my need for her grows until I feel it cannot be contained, much like the beast. If he wants something enough, he will come to the forefront and take control. I know he wants Elle enough, and can sense, without understanding the complexity of our situation, what having her will do for him.

For both of us.

I breathe through the nearly overwhelming urge to pin her and lick her and have her. To remind her that she is already claimed. Mine. She is mine. Possessiveness surges through me.

Elle leans forward, pressing her body closer to me.

Another sharp wave of lust steals my breath. It is not mine alone, but Elle's, too. My mind fills with questions. Is it the power of the magic? Is it the forbidden?

Or is it something else?

CHAPTER 15

THE PRINCE AND THE BEAST

It feels dangerous. The rush of adrenaline heats my entire being. This time, the beast does not go back to his resting state. Not with her so close, so obedient, and so fucking beautiful. The beast stretches himself out, his power filling my chest and making my lust more palpable by far. The light caresses her cheek and I find myself obsessed with this moment. For years I have wanted nothing as much as I want her right now.

The sight of the moon spurs me to action. Its pull is as undeniable as it was when I took Elle from her father's house.

With clear sight of the moon and with everything I have done with Elle, from watching her take in the ballroom by moonlight to feeling the vibration of her moans around my fingers as I fed her, the beast has far more demands and I find myself more and more willing to allow the primal needs power over me.

And the scent of her is even stronger. Telling her I would require her obedience has made her heart thud and the slightest sheen of sweat appear on her skin. I did not know that one woman could be both salty and sweet and desirous and nervous all at the same time.

There are many things that affect how I feel about the woman who sits close enough for me to grasp her throat in my hand without leaning in to reach it. The moon has just begun to wane from the full, so its influence is still incredibly strong. The castle has been a magical place for many years, and the magic of the curse interacts with it. Include the moon, which tugs at my spirit, and all make the beast powerful and hungry.

But maybe it is just Elle.

Maybe it is just her that gives me this swelling sense of need and possession. Maybe I would have felt the same about her if I'd come across her at a ball with all the townspeople in attendance. Maybe I'd have felt the same if I rode through the village and met her eyes outside the bakery where she worked.

I reach for my goblet of wine and bring it to my lips. I serve Elle nothing but the finest wine and feed her nothing but the finest foods, and so the wine has a deep, rich flavor that bursts with sweetness and tannins on my tongue. The taste reminds me of long-ago glasses of wine in crowded dining rooms, the high energy of couples whirling across the dance floor saturating the space, and the air thick with laughter and flirtatious murmurs and greetings between friends. It warms me as it goes down.

The longing is nothing compared to my longing for her.

I take her chin in my hand the way I fantasized about only minutes ago and stroke her cheek with the pad of my thumb.

Elle opens her mouth with a sudden gasp, her lips and tongue glistening in the firelight. It may be my imagination, but a beam of moonlight falls across her mouth as well, bending my attention toward it. The same beam of moonlight winks on the goblet in my hand.

I raise it to her lips with meticulous care. Elle breathes shallowly as the goblet nears her lips as if she can sense it. Perhaps the scent or even the faintest of sound warns her.

I guide the goblet to her bottom lip. She closes her mouth over the rim, lifting her chin slightly but waiting for a word from me. My cock strains achingly against my breeches.

"Drink," I order her in a low voice.

Elle drinks with tentative sips, but a droplet of wine slips out from between her lips and dribbles down her chin. She pulls back slightly from the goblet, offering me a view of her face. The drop of wine drips off the elegant point of her chin and lands on her chest, trailing into her cleavage.

With a roar that I manage to subdue into a growl when it

tears through my throat, the beast lunges, pushing me out of his way in a frenzy of lust.

Eager to lick the wine from her chin and continue to devour her bit by bit.

To my surprise, a small moan escapes Elle. She leans closer to me, and I wrestle for space with the beast, both of us reaching for her.

She's as turned on as I am. My beauty is in need. The lust and desire are thick between us, and I cave like the mere mortal I am.

I pull her out of her chair and between my legs, sitting up straight so I can lick the wine from between her breasts. I hardly notice the dishes from the meal and the platters of food flying from the room in an orderly row, granting us space to consume one another.

It is only one drop of wine, but it tastes as heavenly as the longer sip I drank before, made better by the sweetness of her skin. I follow the trail up to Elle's chin and lick the evidence there, too, finally capturing her mouth. She whimpers into the kiss, but it is not a plea to stop. On the contrary, she presses herself between my legs with more force.

Fuck. She makes it both harder for me to fight the beast and harder to discern between the two of us.

I take her by the hips and guide her over my thigh. I do not know whether it is me or the beast who pushes her blue dress up to her hips. And I don't give a fuck so long as she's bared to me. She wears nothing underneath, and I press one of my hands into each of her thighs, my mind swallowed up by the heat of her pussy against me. Elle arches, rolling her hips, trying to get contact. I suckle at her neck, tasting her pulse and the magic and moonlight in a thick haze around us.

I had a mind to wait, to perhaps coax her into accepting me into her body, but a demanding growl vibrates through my chest. My memories crowd into my mind, both as I remember them and as the beast remembers them, which is tinged with strong scents and stronger feelings untainted by the rules and morals I was raised with. The beast is a creature of the wild, a dark, magical forest where the choice is between eating and being eaten, claiming or having the object of one's desires claimed by a stronger predator.

There is no stronger predator, and the beast has run out of patience.

Or perhaps it is me who has run out of patience, and the line between us is too blurred for me to feel who is to blame.

In one smooth movement, I push her off my thigh and turn her, bending her over the table. Her small hands slap the wood as she finds her position. I take her waist in one hand and again push her dress higher to her waist. A man in possession of himself would likely pull it over her head, protecting the fine fabric, but I do not care to protect such luxuries.

And the man I have become enjoys the sight of crumpled silk in uneven lines over her slim waist. Elle arches her back, her palms flat against the table, the blindfold falling down her skin in a line of black silk that stands out against the blue.

It takes a single touch at her gorgeous, shapely thighs for Elle to spread them. She rises on tiptoes, her feet slipping out of the slippers. The next time I readjust my stance I hit one with my foot, and it slides beneath the table. I do not care to see it again. I only care to get my hand between her thighs and stroke flesh I know will already be sodden.

She is as wet and ready as she was in the bed and lifts her hips into my touch, moaning softly. Elle moves, and I glance up to see that she has pillowed her arms on the table and leans her forehead in, seeming lost in the sensation of my touch, though I have given her only one stroke. I drag three fingers through her sweet arousal again, teasing at her opening and then searching out the swollen nub of her clit. Desire builds as I listen to her moans grow louder and her thighs begin to tremble with her impending orgasms.

My pulse beats in my ears, a feeling of deep shame surfacing and falling away. The terms I offered Elle were selfish, but the way I drag pleasure out of her is even more so. I want to sink in her and be enveloped by the evidence of her desire. I want her to work her hips back to take more of my cock, her hunger to be stoked higher than any fire in the castle.

Elle cries out, lifting her head, her back a beautiful arch amid the wrinkled silk of her dress. I release her hip and shove her dress higher until I can see the delicate curves of her shoulder blades working as she rides out an intense orgasm. I recognize the pitch of Elle's voice as she moans, beginning to come down.

She wants more pleasure.

"Yes," I say, half to her and half to myself, guilt at my selfishness mixing with the unavoidable sense of relief. She is enjoying it. She wants me. She *needs* me even. My body has ached for this, and the beast has snapped and growled for this since we came upon Elle sitting in that swing, the shawl around her shoulders. "*Yes.*"

I bend over her, my hand working once again over her clit. Elle throws her head back as I fold myself over her and lick the side of her neck. I find the place on her shoulder where I bit her before and press my teeth into the flesh, drawing a gasp from Elle that turns into a low moan. She begins to come again on my fingers, her pussy so hot and wet that moving my fingers at all causes them to enter her. Elle thrusts her hips back, taking two of my fingers inside her, and I push in, pressing and stretching into her to prepare her for what's to come.

She clenches sweetly around my knuckles, her channel tight and hot and responsive. Elle moves her hips with more urgency now and I put my hand on her hip again, holding her in place where I want her while still allowing her to rock on my fingers. Each gasp that slips from between her lips is answered with a soft whimper or moan. None of her sounds form words, but the plea is clear enough.

I need her higher. The angle of the table is not right for me to fuck her bent this way, so I take her hips in both my hands and lift her. Elle scrambles onto the table on all fours, her dress falling around her shoulders. When she regains her balance, she tips her head back again, her hair and the black silk of the blindfold spilling over her back.

Fucking gorgeous.

I fumble for the ties of my breeches, nearly snapping them in my haste. The laces come undone under fingers that feel more like the beast's than my own. I plunge my hand into my gaping breeches and take out my cock. It's hard and pulsing, already leaking precum at the tip, and I drag it through Elle's folds, trying to steady my breath.

She makes a low, pleading sound, pushing her hips back into my hand. Though she has come twice, her opening still feels tight, and I position the head of my cock at her center. The feeling of her hot, wet pussy against my skin is almost enough to bring me to orgasm before I've entered her. My vision darkens under a wave of pleasure I am granted only by touching her and feeling her slick warmth coat the head of my cock. I have been isolated for so long that even with wringing pleasure out of her earlier, I still crave it like nothing I've ever desired before.

Elle wriggles her bottom, arching lower so her opening begins to take in the head of my cock. I release a groan that turns into a growl, fighting for control. The animal in me wants to pin her roughly to the table and fuck into her deeply and mercilessly, showing her once and for all who has dominion over her body, but the prince in me, turned beastly by so many years of loneliness, desperately wants to be inside her, lost in the presence of a pure, innocent heart.

Of course I want to claim her, too. Of course I want to show her how she belongs to me.

I push forward, enveloping myself only an inch. Elle gasps and throws her head back again but this time her fists clench. *Her first. Her only.* I savor the moment. I bury my fist in the dress at her back, catching the blindfold, and hold tight, not pulling hard because I do not want any damage done to her delicate neck but adding tension to keep the intoxicating arch of her body where I want it. Elle trembles, her hands opening and closing on the table, and pants, her cunt fluttering around me with every breath she takes.

I place both my hands on her hips and push forward one more inch, drawing another gasp from her lips. Her whimper is delectable.

The feel of her is so tight and so hot, surrounding my cock in the sweetest flesh I could have imagined, and I manage to take her slowly one more inch before I can no longer hold the beast at bay. I do not know if I am even trying when he seizes control of my body and drives into Elle, sheathing my cock to the hilt.

Elle leans into it, bracing herself as much as she can

against the table, her cries and moans echoing in the room as I fuck her ruthlessly. Her pussy ripples as she orgasms again.

Her skin is already reddened underneath my fingertips. There will be bruises when I am finished, but I cannot stop. I do not want to stop. I want her here with me, claimed, marked with my seed. The beast urges my body into Elle, his vision narrowed to her lithe frame on the table and the pool of silk around her.

My cock pulses as I near my release. Elle moans and cries but does not pull away. She moves her hips back, trying to take more of me, though I am already buried in her as deeply as I will go, and her body cannot accept more.

I would never have thought she would bend so easily and accept my girth with cries of pleasure. I can hardly see when she clenches down around me, so tight my cock is nearly strangled. I pulse inside her, my length growing thicker, and I cannot stop the feral growls that issue from between my teeth. There is no point in battling the beast now. He has taken over fully and will not be sated again until he has had his fill, and I am too caught up in Elle's pleasure to care.

My release erupts out of me with a cry that shakes the castle. Elle's cunt milks me until the last of my hot release has spilled deep inside her. I emerge slowly from the depths of pleasure.

I made bruises on her skin.

When I can see well enough, they stand out, stark on her

hips. My vision continues to clear as the beast pulls back, content on claiming our beauty.

The mess of Elle on the table, my release dripping from between her legs tinged with blood from her virginity, is like a sword to the chest. As my selfish satisfaction grows, so does my guilt. The two sensations are like the prince and the beast, jostling for space and never having enough for the two of them. Because there is only one body. There is only one way to be righteous and moral and it is not to be a beast, yet I have no choice and cannot think of anything else when the scent of her is all over me and her pleasure is heavy in the room.

What have I done?

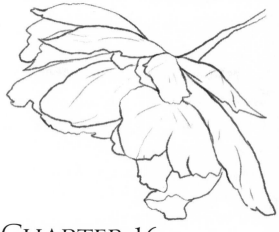

CHAPTER 16

ELLE

I've never felt so light and yet so heavy. So at peace and ease and yet consciously aware of what's been done and what cannot be taken back. I'm warm everywhere in my body when the beast pulls away. The feeling of hot, wet release between my legs captures all my attention for a moment and I struggle to catch my breath. My muscles shake, overwhelmed by the sheer amount of sensation he poured into me. It is hard to think in this state, but gradually I become aware that he is breathing roughly, as if something's wrong.

Magic instantly surrounds me, soothing the thought out of my mind. He cannot have been unhappy, because I heard the sounds he made as he took me as well. I heard the relief hidden in the feral growls. It was as if he had been caged for many years and had finally been set free.

I will admit, I feel the same. The pulsing pleasure that remains between my legs feels entirely new and I am relieved, though it takes me several moments to figure out why.

The beast has claimed me.

Oddly, my lips are lulled into a contented smile. As if my dreams came true. As if this was all supposed to happen.

Bit by bit the memories are etched into my mind and replayed. He licked the wine from my chin and my chest, nipping at my skin. They were not bites like he gave me on the swing to leave marks but almost as if to explore. I felt his control snap when he began to push into me, and I felt the expectation of my life in the village break away from me at that moment as well. I didn't ever expect to behave so wantonly even in my marriage bed, and I cannot think of a man in the village who would have turned me so desperate and seeking the way the beast has.

His knuckles brush the inside of my thigh and move up through the mess he's made of me, settling one more time at my pussy. My heart races in anticipation, still unable to see and not knowing what happens next. The beast makes an even rougher sound, then hisses as if he has discovered someone else's wrongdoing.

I do not know what it means. My lack of experience and naivety play tricks on me. Doubting what I feel. Denying the pull as some foolish thought.

When he kissed me, I felt that we were both giving in to the magic and the tension between us. There may have been shame in that before but there can't be any now.

A cloth presses gently between my legs, cleaning up some of the mess, and then the beast pulls my dress down. His gentle touch is at odds with how he just was. He takes me by the waist, avoiding the places where his fingers dug into my hips before, and lifts me down from the table. I'm barefooted, and I cannot say where my house slippers are.

I start to ask if he knows where they are or if he wants me to find them and sway instead, overwhelmed by the pleasure and the food and the late hour. I have to brace myself. My eyes begin to close behind the blindfold, which has managed to stay in place while the beast had his way with me. I can still feel him...and something else. Something that pulls me into a deep slumber.

The last thing I am aware of is being carried in a strong pair of arms and a blanket being pulled over me before I fall into a deep, dreamless sleep.

Days go by, and they are nothing like the night I arrived in the castle.

I wake in an empty bed with sunlight streaming through

the window. No notes appear on the floor instructing me what to wear. There are underthings in the wardrobe and any dress I wear is cleaned and hung to wear again while I am asleep.

It is pleasant most places in the castle, but I do not see the beast.

I waited for him the first morning, but after breakfast appeared on a tray in my room and I've eaten and explored every inch of the room I know best, I decide to venture out. And what a sight it all is to behold. I am bewitched by the estate.

The castle is large and I move slowly through the hall outside my bedroom, looking at all that I could not see the first night I was here. The blindfold made that impossible, although night would not have been the best time to observe the halls. There is much to see in any castle, I suppose, but this one is carefully decorated without being crowded. I pause before each painting and look at them with the same sense of awe I had in the ballroom.

They're breathtaking. The details and finery. It was once said that he had destroyed every ounce of beauty and the magic cast darkness in every corner. They were lies I was told. For there is nothing but beauty and life in every inch of this place.

When a day comes and goes with no sign of the beast, I find my bed turned down and the candles low in the room. A hot mug of chamomile tea waits on my bedside table. It soothes me into another deep sleep. It is never cold the way it was when I slept in my father's cottage. I do not wake in the night shivering, pulling a thin blanket around me. I have pleasant dreams of being full of delicious food and lulled by the weight of a fine comforter, and I wake with the sun in my window and the fire still crackling in the grate.

Although I do worry about my father and what he thinks. He has no idea where I've gone. And I have no idea what has happened in my absence.

I go a second day without seeing the beast or any sign of him. I do not hear his footsteps following me in the hall. I do not hear him commanding any of the castle's objects to work.

He's nowhere to be found and that makes me anxious. I can't fight the turmoil that brews inside.

I begin to wonder if I misinterpreted the things we did on the dining room table. I find the room itself and look in, but there is nothing to suggest he fucked me atop the table after feeding me from his hand. It is a gorgeous dining room with heavy, expensive furniture, but he is not waiting there for me.

That night the beast seemed different, almost unable to stop touching me, unable to stop kissing me or licking the wine from my body. He seemed driven to have me by something stronger than magic, and I felt the same. He kissed me and fucked me with such ferocity that at times I wondered if he had lost control to the urges of his body, which I would not have minded.

It meant something to me that I cannot place...but I have no idea what it meant to him.

I'm left to my own thoughts, looking at a large painting of a grand battle scene with knights on horseback valiantly charging into the fray. Those whose faces are visible look courageous and determined. Am I like those knights, or is it the beast who is determined?

Perhaps it is both of us.

It cannot have been an accident, however. He took me from my father's house and brought me here, for I cannot have passed through the wall and gotten myself through the forest alone without waking.

Although there were those vines in the trees, wrapping around my ankle and pulling me...

No, I think there would have been evidence of that. Scratches from tree branches and bruised toes, and I have neither. Right? My sanity plays tricks on me.

So he cannot have made a mistake. What happened was not a mistake, I'm sure. I felt his mouth, hot and desperate on mine, and it was not the touch of a man who wanted to be doing something else.

I do not know what went wrong. I do not know what has made him retreat into silence and avoid me. It is not difficult in a castle this size, but why would he want to?

He told me to obey him, and I did so with almost ease and enjoyment, because his kiss made me want more. If I had shown that I was not willing, I think he would have drawn back. I did not feel any hesitation that night, save for a little when I woke up and found myself in a castle far from home. The question of whether it was the magic or his presence that made me feel that way seems almost irrelevant, but as the day stretches on and I do not see him, my thoughts return to the topic again and again.

I nearly debate leaving. Simply walking out of the gate. But fear keeps me from testing that boundary. That and my promise that I would stay. If I were to go back home, Crawe may be waiting for me. They will need answers as to what's happened.

My heart races with endless possibilities of the tragedy that may occur either way. Along with the judgment and penalties for what I've done.

The moment the sadness consumes me and my thoughts travel down that round, the magic pulls me somewhere else in the castle. With trinkets I've only heard of before, I'm suddenly swept away into wonderment.

There is little else to think of. I am relatively free within the castle. It's peaceful and quiet aside from the movements of the objects that dust and mop in the rooms and halls closest to mine. Every morning, the bed I am sleeping in remakes itself with fresh sheets, the fabric hovering over the mattress. The pillows fluff themselves. The comforter smooths itself out and tucks itself in tight as if done by the most experienced housekeeper. In the afternoons, the floor is swept by a broom that dances over the floors. I see this happen in other bedrooms, sheets snapping and flying and tucking themselves into mattresses, each room seeming to prepare for something, though no one arrives.

I do not think anyone else lives here. I do not see servants or housekeepers or footmen. For all the motion in the castle keeping it perfectly clean, it begins to seem quite empty.

I explore the long hallways. Some doors open as I approach, inviting me in to see the trinkets or antiques that lay within. They are dark and dusty, these rooms, but when I walk in and imagine them cleaned and bright, the house springs to life again. Windows open, letting in fresh air and closing themselves before they make the rooms uncomfortably cold. Brooms appear to take the dust from the floors.

Where is the beast? Where has he gone?

I do not think he has left the castle, but if he has, I do not think I can go after him. He has forbidden me from leaving. I think stepping away from the castle grounds would be obvious disobedience, and I would not be able to get a message to my father, nor convince the beast to send one.

Have I imagined the beast?

For a little while, I wonder if I've made all this up in my mind. It could be that I wanted to escape Crawe so badly that I've fallen into a dream and can't be woken. Maybe I'm lying in my bed at my father's cottage right now, my father leaning over me, worriedly trying to wake me.

But then that cannot be. Just as the scar from the beast's

bite mark still lingers on my shoulder, the bruises he pressed into my hips also linger. I check for them each morning in the mirror and while they are beginning to fade away, I can still see them. I can feel the echoes of the friction between us and the heat of him inside me.

In the afternoons I look at more paintings or curl up in a chair by a fireplace, relishing the peace. This life is one I've never felt before. Sleeping with ease and worrying for nothing...apart from my father. It was not often in the village that I was able to take time for myself after reaching womanhood. My father needed all the money I could earn, which was not much but it kept us from starving.

In the castle, I have no fear of starving. My breakfast appears each morning in my room, and lunch appears wherever I happen to be in the castle, usually on a convenient table with a chair and a window to look out of. The same goes for dinner. Everything I am served is as fine as the food the beast fed me, but it does not have quite the same appeal as when I was able to suck it off his fingers.

On the third day I find the kitchen.

It is late afternoon, and the light is golden in the spacious kitchen equipped to feed ballrooms full of people. The light falls on sturdy countertops, gleaming copper pots, and rows of polished knives and ladles and serving forks.

It comes to life as I enter, the tea kettle jumping on the stove. As I wander nearer to a pair of wide sinks, they turn on, spilling clear water below. I rinse my hands in the water, finding it pleasantly cool. On the window ledge, a small, lush herb garden grows, the plants fragrant. When I reach to touch the carved wood of the box, a watering can floats from its hook, fills itself with water at the sink, and sprinkles water over the herbs.

It entertains me, the magic does. I'm entranced by it and all it does.

On one shelf, I find a row of cookbooks. Some are heavy and ornate, while others are smaller and worn. I choose one of the ones that looks loved and open the leather cover. The pages have illustrations here and there and finally the cookbook falls open to a recipe for a fruit tart.

I place my finger on the page, thinking to read through the list of ingredients, but at my touch cabinets open with a *bang*, startling me. I drop the cookbook to the countertop and whirl to discover what's happening.

Various cabinets open and items fly out. A bowl spins to a stop on the huge island at the center of the kitchen. An icebox opens and fruits soar out, arranging themselves next to the bowl. Sugar and butter float from somewhere nearby. My heart races as I realize what's happening. I turn back to the cookbook and stare at the list of ingredients.

Before long the kitchen has gathered everything necessary to make the fruit tart. I watch in astonishment as dough is prepared and rolled out and settled into a circular tin. The filling mixes itself together with plenty of sugar, the white grains coating the fruit. I think of Ara at the bakery, her hands red and sore from the work she begins before sunrise and of how much time this would save her.

Would this magic work outside of the castle? How far can the magic go? I do not know, and I watch, entranced, as the oven glows brighter and the prepared tart floats inside.

I've heard of witches...perhaps an essence remains. I do not know, but my mind wanders as the kitchen utensils move around me.

The light begins to fade as the sun sets, glowing orange through the window. It finishes sinking into the horizon as the tart pops from the oven and floats to a rack to cool. Candles burn to life in sconces on the walls, illuminating the kitchen with comforting light.

That is when I hear footsteps in the hall.

They pause outside the door, then enter, but I keep my eyes on the window as they move across the room. I think the beast is moving behind a wall that leads to a large pantry.

My breath quickens and I stay perfectly still. I haven't got my blindfold with me. I wait for a command, finding myself hoping that it is him. Realizing just how lonely I've been without him.

It is darker on that end of the kitchen, and my heart races. I want to turn and search for his eyes in the shadows, but I do not. The last rays of the sun fade, and nervousness sets in. I have come to the kitchen without permission. The beast did not forbid me from coming here, but he did not permit it, either. There have been no notes on the bedroom floor telling me where to go or what to wear, but that does not mean he has no thoughts about it. And now I have had the house prepare a tart from his stores.

"I'm sorry," I say, my voice soft but seeming loud in the kitchen after days of quiet. "I didn't know—"

"Do not be," the beast answers before I can finish my apology. "It pleases me that you make yourself comfortable."

Releasing a breath I didn't know I was holding, I move to the counter, and the tart slides off the rack and settles itself in the space next to it. It's a perfect fruit tart. When I hover my hand above it, I find it has cooled enough to cut. A knife presents itself as soon as I have the thought and cuts the tart into even pieces. Two small plates float from the cupboard and arrange themselves on the counter as well, and dessert forks follow them, along with a small serving fork, which plates a slice of tart on each of the plates.

"Would you like some?" I ask, my heart thundering. The beast's presence in the kitchen is heady and makes me wish he was closer, yet I know I cannot approach him. I can almost smell the masculine scent of him, and it fills my mind with more questions. I press my lips shut and do not ask them.

There is a pause as he considers. "Do not attempt to look when I'm behind you," he commands.

I nod, already imagining that would be a request, and fix my eyes firmly on the window. His footsteps draw nearer and my heart beats even harder. One of the plates slides off the counter, and I finally lower my eyes to the plates and pick up my fork and take a bite.

Heat takes over my body and the closer he gets, the higher the temperature. My body begs for me to bow to him, to plead with him for a kiss or for his touch. But I stay calm and wait. Merely taking the smallest bite of the tart.

The tart is a perfect balance of the sweetness of fruit and sugar, but as I swallow, my chest aches.

Is this my destiny? To be alone with the magic and the beast forever? I did not think that was what he meant that night in the dining room, and now I think it must be.

Silver clinks on china behind me. I take another bite, trying to keep my breathing steady. It is hard to swallow, and maybe that's what make me brave enough to speak.

"Will you come during the day?" I ask, my voice steadier than I feel but still soft and hopeful. "If I promise I will not look?"

There is silence, and my heart sinks. If this is one of the questions he does not want to answer...

"Are you lonely?" comes his deep voice.

"Yes," I admit, the pang in my chest even stronger.

He inhales. "Not as lonely as I."

I do not know how to answer him without asking more questions. I think if I were to press, then he would stay silent, and if he stays silent and refuses to speak to me at all, the silence might be worse than wandering alone through the halls.

His plate clicks on the counter. I do not look at it but set my own plate down. A single glance tells me that the beast's plate is empty. Mine is still almost full.

"Let me show you the library," he says.

The beast guides me through the halls with a light touch on the small of my back, but this time he does not blindfold me. I keep my eyes forward, resisting the urge to lean into his touch and turn toward him, seeing his face at last.

A set of double doors opens before us and the beast guides me into the largest library I have ever seen. It must be as tall as the castle itself and is no less grand than the ballroom. Paintings cover the ceiling with gold glinting in the candlelight. Heavy shelves hold hundreds and hundreds of books. Only someone with unimaginable wealth would be able to afford this many books and a room such as this to keep them in.

I do not even know what the cost would be or if the village combined could afford such luxury.

"May I..." My voice shakes, forcing me to start again. "May I come here often?"

"You may roam all you wish apart from the highest floor of the tower."

I have not gone there yet. There is much in the castle to explore, and the tower did not call to me. If I felt anything, it was a quiet suggestion to stay away.

"What is there?" I ask, my eyes tracing the spines of the books on the nearest shelf.

"None of your concern."

I hold my breath, waiting to see if he will continue, or if he will touch me, or hold me, or perhaps even kiss me, but after a silence thick with tension, his footsteps retreat toward the door and fade away, making it feel even more quiet.

When I finally brave a glance behind me, the beast has gone.

CHAPTER 17

THE PRINCE AND THE BEAST

The highest floor of the tower is the place in the castle where the darkness dwells most deeply.

I know that the people in the village gossip about the darkness that has enveloped this place, and there is some truth to those tales. In the first days after the witch cast her curse, the darkness from the storm of her magic seeped into the walls and clouded all the windows, making it dark as night outside even when the sun was high. It drove me to madness; I'm sure of it.

Gradually, as the years passed, that darkness faded. No villagers tried to breach the walls after the mob came after me and failed to kill me, but I assume the rumors stayed stuck in their minds as rumors tend to do.

No, the castle is not shrouded in darkness completely, though the mist still clings in the enchanted forest and my forced solitude has felt like darkness at times. There are parts of the castle that have fallen out of my mind, unvisited for years in a row. I have no knowledge of their state. There have been many days when it did not seem worth the effort of getting out of my bed and the castle may as well have been as dark as the stories say.

In this room, the darkness is real.

It is not a space meant to be seen by visitors, and so is not finely decorated, though the circular room contains carpets and a table and a chair that is well-enough built. On the table sits the glass cloche that contains the rose that bears the remnants of the curse, just as I do. Because of the nature of it, darkness crowds the room like a tapestry on the walls, translucent but not transparent, making the moonlight from the waning crescent seem dimmer and less potent.

I have grown used to the darkness over the years, and even become accustomed to the fact that the rose and its petals are here, a physical representation of what remains of my life.

Staring at the rose in its cloche feels different now.

I sit back in the chair with a sigh and let my eyes linger on the rose as if I have never seen it before. The stem has not changed in appearance since the day the witch cursed me, and the petals are as pink as if freshly bloomed. Its physical state has not changed much since the day I dragged myself back to the castle, beaten and bleeding, and brought myself to this tower to lie on the floor until I could summon the strength to pull myself upright and go down to my bed chambers. I know that must seem senseless, but at the time, in the haze of my wounds, I thought that proximity to the rose would help with the healing. To this day, I have no idea whether it made any difference at all. I only know that climbing the tower steps nearly killed me and when I arrived here, I thought the tower walls would be the last thing I saw before I died.

Clouds must cover the moon, because the light coming through the tower window dims further. The glass still shines, as there is much magic in the tower and the cloche and, of course, the rose itself. It is as if the moonlight is stored within the glass and twinkles whenever the moon itself is not strong enough to shine off it. It makes it difficult to look away from the rose and remember my sentence.

No magic will save me. That has been obvious for a long time. Magic can only extend the curse, in its way, since without magic I would have starved to death or bled to death many times over by now. I have been under this curse for twenty long years. I have been battling the beast for what feels like an eternity, unable to stray far from the castle, as the magic weakens with distance and cannot protect me as I need, even in the village.

The truth is that it is the isolation that blackens my soul

far more than the curse. It turns me into a man I do not recognize, even accounting for the beast that steals half my waking hours and perhaps more. The loneliness has been like a noose around my neck, and now I feel I have slipped out of it. Yet there it hangs, for me to witness.

But now Elle is here, and the castle is no longer empty. I can feel her presence through the beast's senses and the magic of the castle. Her bright spirit is undimmed by sleep, and she slumbers deeply in her bedroom, safe under the covers while I am up here with the rose.

As I watch, one of the petals trembles on the stem as if stirred by a breeze that only moves within the cloche. It is such a small movement that a man without the beast's senses might think he had imagined it, but I know I have not. It may not be the first sign that another petal is about to fall, but it is the first one I have seen from this petal, and I know well enough what will happen in due course.

Many years ago, I used to believe that the act of looking is what hastened the petals in falling to the bottom of the cloche, but that was a superstitious thought and one that I eventually stopped having. If it were real, I could stave off the effects of the rose seemingly forever, simply by locking it in a room deep within the castle and never allowing it to see the light of day.

That is not how it works. Whether I look or not, time still passes. What I do in that time is irrelevant to the state of the clock ticking. The petals will still fall. Watching the rose for hours a day does not seem to make a difference. Ignoring the rose for weeks at a time makes no difference. Consideration alone does not affect the curse.

And yet, on nights like these, I find myself before it. I do not find the rose to be entrancing or alluring. At one time I may have looked at the rose the way a solider will look at a wound that cannot be healed but will not cause a mercifully quick death.

The petal quivers again in such a slight motion that I almost allow myself to hope it will not fall. When I was first cursed, it would have been a simple matter to convince myself that it had not moved at all and forbid myself from looking for a month, but now I cannot lie to myself. Elle has changed everything.

Despite my determination to be stoic, the sight of another quivering petal turns my stomach to knots.

I follow the line of the stem to the bottom of the cloche. I do not try to convince myself that the number of petals is unchanged, because every time I come to this room in the tower, the number of petals that have fallen is burned freshly into my memory. I cannot lie to myself about this, either. There are more petals on the bottom of the glass cloche than there were the last time I was here.

Try as I might, I cannot remember when that was. It was before I brought Elle to the castle, but how long before?

When I search my memories, I cannot recall how the land looked outside the window or whether there was rain drumming on the roof. I cannot remember if it was dark out or daylight. I cannot remember if it was hot or cold. It makes me feel crazed.

I cannot even remember whether it was this year or last, or even the year before. There have been times in my life when the days blurred together with no way to tell them apart. The beast and I fought for control and space in my body, and the hours passed without notice as I struggled to force him into submission or retreated into my mind and let him run loose when I was too exhausted to keep up the fight.

Other times, though, the years were interminable, each day stretching out until I thought for sure a week had passed, only to find that the sun had not yet set. My mind remained clear during those days, and I dwelled in overwhelming anguish and pain and guilt thinking back to the day the witch came to the castle.

It was too late when she arrived. There was not time to build a wall and keep her out, or to gather any weaponry that could hope to overpower her. There had not been any warning signs, and her arrival was an ambush. All I could do was flee the castle with the people who dwelled there. I gathered as many as I could, every servant I could find, as the witch swept into the castle, and we ran through the forest to the village. The journey seemed never-ending. There was not room for all of us in the inn so we divided ourselves among the homes of the villagers who would take us in.

At first the villagers were welcoming, as they understood the fear of having to flee from a sudden attack. We had escaped with our lives, the most precious thing to defend, and for a short while it seemed as if that would be the worst of it. Perhaps the witch would pass on and we could go back to the comfort of the castle.

I should have known then that we had not run far enough and the witch would never give up the castle without being completely defeated. Black clouds darkened the sky. They were like nothing we had ever seen, swirling in vicious spirals above the village. They cracked open with brutal lightning that set trees on fire and split the earth. It was a warning of what was to come.

At the time I could not understand how it had happened. Dark witches are normally handled by their own kind. They keep each other in line, for their power is too great to be challenged by most others. I had not been prepared for such an attack and I did not have an enchantress at the castle. There was not even a wise woman in the village who could offer the slightest protection.

The storm raged above the village for three days and three nights, and I began to understand that it would not stop without my intervention. I resisted the idea because I did not want to face the witch in a place of power, but when yet another house was struck down by lightning and the inhabitants ran screaming from the flames, I knew I had to act. The people were mine to protect and my cowardice was the cause of their pain.

The townspeople did not have the means to fight the dark witch and her magic. Neither did I, but I was the only one among us valuable enough to speak with her. No one else had more power or standing than I did. Although I asked my closest allies if they would come with me, they wished to stay behind. I could not blame them. As I would learn, she had come for me.

There was no wall then, so I crossed through the trees on the way back to the castle. My home had been turned dark and forbidding by the witch's magic. The clouds followed me through the forest and spiraled above the castle. My heart thundered. I could hardly breathe when I reached the entrance of the castle and went inside.

I found the witch in this very spot, the highest floor of the tower. From here you can see the slope of the forest toward the village and the smoke from the houses rising into the sky. You can see the green country beyond. The witch had taken my power over that country for herself and turned with a gleeful smile as I came into the tower. I could see from her twisted features that she was satisfied with the fear she was causing to my people.

"Well, little prince," she said. "Have you come to bargain?"

I am not little now, and I was not little then, but I was the prince. I straightened my shoulders and my spine. "Yes."

She smiled, slow and deadly. "What do you have to offer me? I have already taken your home and your power. I have driven away your people and could chase them even farther, if I chose."

I knew at that moment that she was right and would take pleasure in terrorizing my people until they were too afraid to ever return to this countryside. She would have no qualms about destroying the village next just to hear the screams of the people who lived there. She was in control of my treasury and all my gold as well as my stores. She already had the power that surrounded such places, like royal castles, and allowed us to live in comfort, and she would take more until there was no more to take. The only thing she did not have at that point was me.

"I will trade myself," I said.

I had almost expected her to refuse, to tell me that I was not worth the bargain, but instead the witch beamed as if I was offering her something truly rare. Indeed, I did not understand fully what she meant to do with me. I thought death. An ending to the pain. I was a fool.

The story that the villagers tell is that I was fed to the beast, but the truth is that it was the other way around. He was fed to me, forced into my body from one of my own goblets. The edge of the cup cut into my mouth. I did not want to drink the bitter liquid that she had made from wine from my own cellars, but I had no other choice if the village was to be saved.

"A sip," she said, and I dared to believe it would end the misery. As if a soul like hers could have mercy.

The curse burned inside me. I remember the sound of the witch laughing wickedly, louder and louder. Her laughter blended in with the thunder and cracks of lightning from the clouds she had summoned. She was triumphant, and I thought for a few moments that it had all been a waste because as the curse took hold, I felt as if I was being torn in two. I was sickened by the magic itself and fell to the ground in a delirium.

When I awoke three days later, the witch's reign had already ended. Her greed had been her undoing. The other witches, who would have stopped her from seizing the castle at all, had heard what their sister had done. I have a faint memory of her screams as they bound her in the courtyard and lit her aflame, extinguishing her evil soul.

The damage had already been done.

I was doomed to a life of madness and animal urges. In the beginning, the beast was stronger and I was less able to fight him. The magic would enforce the power of the rose.

So long ago, I did not think of what would happen when the last petal fell. I thought I would go mad long before then.

In time, I've realized I might live long enough to see the

last petal fall from the rose. "If you do not find your fate before the last petal falls...you will become nothing but the beast inside of you." The witch had warned.

Of course I did not give up so easily then. I raged through the castle destroying tapestries and paintings and vases for days until I could control the beast. When I finally trusted myself enough, I was covered in sweat and weaker than I had ever been, but with the last of my strength I dragged myself outside.

The wall had been built by magic while I was inside the castle. It was too large and too sturdy to have been built by human hands and had the scent of magic about it. I thought it had been built to keep the villagers away, to protect them from me, but once I passed through I began to reconsider. The magic was weaker outside the iron gates, and I felt weaker as I walked. By the time I reached the village I knew I had made a terrible mistake.

The villagers were terrified of me. They did not trust me and looked upon me as a dangerous animal who could not be allowed to live. There was not only terror, but there was anger and even hate. All they knew of the prince was that he had been fed to the beast, and when I spoke, my words did not fall on their ears as any language they could understand. They had begun to confuse the power of the witch with me, and stories had spread about how I could not be controlled. They had already imagined the worst and turned on me, trying to kill me. They beat me until I was almost senseless and when I ran, trying to get to safety, they chased after me.

Their betrayal was my undoing. Still now, I regret sacrificing myself for their souls.

The magic was too weak near the village to protect me, and I could not defend myself. I barely made it back to the castle, bloodied and terribly injured as I was. The magic inside the castle did its best to help me heal, but as it did, the villagers began storming the estate.

They brought planks and long nails with them, and their plan was to crucify me in my courtyard.

No, that is not true. Their plan was to crucify the beast, and they could not see that I was still part of him. The anger and pain still brew inside of me at the memory. I can still hear the thunder.

I was the only one in the castle by then. There was no one to defend me save myself. I did not want to kill them, but they could not understand me or did not want to. I still remember their screams as they died. I still remember their bravery, fighting to the last man. When the final man had fallen, the women fled to the village. I have no doubt they told the tale of what a vicious animal I was, though I was only trying to stay alive. I know they would not have told the stories in the way I remember it, because all they saw was a bloodthirsty beast.

In fairness, there are days when I am as bloodthirsty as he is because the nature of the beast is overpowering. There are times when I hardly remember my life as it was before I was cursed. Tendrils of darkness swirl through the mists of the forests to this day, and enough of the villagers are aware of them that they look upon those remnants as proof that evil still inhabits the castle.

I blink several times, returning from my memories. On the rose, the petal that had been quivering in that invisible breeze comes loose and floats to the floor of the cloche.

I release a heavy sigh, doing my best to come to terms with my thoughts.

The truth is that I no longer wish to stop the petals from falling. In the early days of the curse, I was so desperate to stop it that I would have held them onto the stem with both my hands, withering away in this tower room. I tossed and turned in bed, trying to find a way to free myself from the curse through the power of my will and finding nothing but dead ends.

Now, I no longer need to search for a way to keep the petals on the stem. It is no longer my most important consideration. I will no longer dwell on the days I have left, for there is no sense in it, and counting them will not change their number.

I will have this peace with Elle for as many days as I can. Numbing my pain. She helps me remember who I used to want to be. I will accept the peace I have with her for that long and no longer, because I will not be here when it is done.

I let out another sigh, stretching my stiff limbs. I cannot go to Elle and wake her without blindfolding her, and I do not want to disturb her pleasant sleep, so I will not. The days I have with her from now until the end will have to be good enough, for there is nothing else to be gained from this life. What's strange, though, is that the magic allows her and no one else. It's odd and I've been trying to understand why it offers her peace. Why it grants her welcome. Is it to further my pain in some way? I can't imagine she is a gift although that's what her presence feels like. I do not trust the magic. None of this feels as though it will stay. It is a trick, I'm sure.

There is only one final question that plagues me as I stand, looking at the cloche in the moonlight, preparing to leave it:

What does the magic want with Elle?

CHAPTER 18

ELLE

I have found the sunniest place in the castle, and it is a grand terrarium that has a large glassed-in ceiling and soaks up all the heat from the sun even in the cold. I've never been in such grandeur.

One morning I wake to sunlight coming in through my bedroom window and miss walking through the brisk air outside. I know I'm missing something that was more a fantasy than anything. Although I had some time to myself, it was occupied more and more by working at the bakery with Ara.

Lately, I have been seeking out the dark, neglected hallways in the castle. I think the magic wants me to stay where the castle is still well-kept, but with so many hours stretching before me, I seek out the places it has *not* been. There are more than I would have guessed at first, but as I wander, asking the castle to clean itself, watching fresh sheets and bedding snap onto beds that can't have been used in many years, it begins to make sense. The beast is only one person. He cannot have used all these rooms, even if he made up some sort of schedule and spent time in each. The castle is large enough that some of the spaces have been covered in the dust and grime of neglect. They've been abandoned and the walls themselves seem to hold pain. Perhaps from the memories of what should have been.

I am finding fewer and fewer of those places now. I have to look harder for the narrow hallways that haven't seen light in too long, and they are quicker to put themselves back in order, as if they have been warned I am coming by the room I've slept in. As if rooms can whisper to each other. What a mad idea. The more I think of it, the more it seems plausible. What else would be happening?

The life where I worked in the bakery with Ara and huddled under my blankets trying to keep warm each night of the winter seems as far away as the dreams I had when I slept in my father's house. Living in a castle was only a fantasy that I never dared to truly entertain because it was never going to happen. I was never going to marry into riches. I was never going to meet a prince, or even a beast. Why would such a person ever notice me?

And now, in this strange twist of fate, I am living in a fairytale. Sometimes it feels as if the castle is the dream and I might wake up at any moment, blinking and trying to warm my fingers before I go to work, knowing that it will be easier to arrive at the bakery early and let my hands warm up while I sweep the floors and prepare the goods for sale.

But though I wake up from many dreams, the castle is not one of them. I wake up warm in my bed every morning under a thick comforter filled with down. Well slept with peace and ease surrounding me. It's so comforting I feel that I cannot trust it.

There is no one else in the castle. It is just me and the beast, still alone, and he does not come to me nearly as much as I wish he would. Even though the two of us are not enough to fill all the emptiness, the castle is alive, and more and more parts of it are returning to how they must have been when there were many people in and out of these rooms and voices filled the halls and servants rushed from place to place, delivering food and clothes and messages.

My bed still makes itself every day, and the room keeps itself fresh, and I am teaching additional rooms to do this every time I wander the halls. I want for almost nothing here. A tray with a delicious breakfast appears in my bedroom every morning and lunches and dinners are no less perfect. If I feel a pang of hunger throughout the day and wonder about tea and biscuits, a tray floats through the door and arranges itself on a nearby table almost before I have finished the thought. No one brings the trays. I have tested this many times, walking around the tray as it floats, waving my hands underneath, and even catching the trays out of the air, but it is truly magic.

Today, on this bright, sunny morning, I work my way through toast dripping with butter, bacon, and honey ham. My father and I could rarely afford these expensive meats after my mother died. We were grateful for the castoffs from the bakery that Ara sometimes let me take. There is fresh fruit dusted with sugar for me as well and eggs that are still hot, as if they have just been tipped out of the pan, though I know they had to travel here from the kitchen somehow.

I think often of my father and how he must be worried. It does not escape me that the magic seems to calm my thoughts when they drift to him. Like a distraction or a sweet little lullaby. I wish it wouldn't. The guilt of being so comfortable consumes me.

When I can't eat another bite, I go to the large bathroom and bathe as the sun streams down, casting reflections of the water on the walls. I have never used such fine soap as I do in the beast's castle. It never chaps my skin and is perfumed with the essence of roses. When I step out of the bath I feel like I've been born into another world and my old life has become a dream.

As I dry myself off and dress for the day, I think of how

easy it is to get used to hot water and fine food. My hair is clean and shiny all the time and when I move it carries the scent of the soap I used.

In a way, my life at the beast's castle is simpler than my life in the village. It was harder when I lived with my father, but I knew the basics would not change. We had to make money. We had to buy food and collect wood for the fire, or else we would starve or freeze.

Here, those worries are nonexistent. There will seemingly always be food whenever I'm hungry, and the fires light themselves. I never have to go collect wood and worry I won't be able to find enough. I don't have to bother with concerns that I'll be hurt somehow, or my father will get injured, and we'll have to make do without one of our paychecks. I'm beginning to think I could read for years and never run out of books in the beast's library, and if I twisted my ankle, the magic would probably send bandages to wrap around it and a cushion to rest it on.

When I am dressed and ready to explore more of the castle, I find myself missing the heat of the summer and the blue skies above and all the green plants that fill the countryside. I had not spent much time in the terrarium because it seemed so alive and not in need of my help to fix itself.

Now I go there simply for the pleasure of it.

The terrarium is larger than the ballroom. It's large enough to fit rows and rows of garden beds built up so I can let my fingertips brush the flowers as I walk through. There are even trees in the terrarium, placed at the corners and throughout the flower beds. It does not remind me of the forest, but perhaps a small orchard without full rows of trees.

It's almost as if I'm walking outside, but there is magic here, too. As I walk, flowers bloom ahead of me, opening as if I'm the sun telling them that it's time to wake up for the day.

I walk through each row, marveling at the many hues of the flowers. Each one has perfect petals, and they seem to open themselves wide and lush as if they want to impress me. These flowers have only ever known this life. They do not find it strange to be pampered in a terrarium. They would probably be happy to be picked by someone passing by and placed in a vase where they could decorate other parts of the castle.

They've never had to worry about birds swooping down from the sky to pluck them away or being stepped on by a woman walking too fast to get to work. They are beautiful, and if I could, I would write about them to my father.

I again feel the twinge of guilt for leaving my father and not pressing the beast to let me contact him. I have to take him at his word, and I feel like my asking would only be answered in silence. I want to tell my father I am well, and there are not many chances to see the beast, so it is almost always on my mind.

My father must be worried. He has to support himself alone and collect firewood and fret about warming the house.

He is older and life has not been kind to his body. He has to put food on the table and probably cannot spare any time to search for me. I hope he does not. I do not know what I would do if my father arrived at the gate looking for me. Would I be able to stay inside? Or would I tell him from within the walls that I do not have to worry about anything but freedom in the beast's castle? There is nothing for me to want other than freedom...although even more than freedom these days, I want company.

How many days have I felt lonely? I have lost track. It is not because my freedom is not important, it just seems... impossible to get it if I want to keep my father safe. And the magic always soothes me if I think about being a prisoner. Or maybe it is the gorgeous clothes and the fine food and the comfortable bed. How can I be a prisoner if I am grateful to exist within these walls?

For this and many reasons, I am more at peace with my capture every day. I do not want to be starving and struggling to stay warm. I have dreamed more than once about having a library like the one in the castle with stories to escape into and imagine another life. I am more accepting now and more at ease, though I cannot explain why and I cannot entirely get rid of the guilt of leaving my father.

As I turn my back to walk down the next row of flowers, footsteps sound in the hall. The beast is a muscled man, from what I have felt, but he is graceful and does not walk with loud footsteps unless he wants to warn me he is coming. His presence immediately fills the terrarium as he steps inside.

My pulse races but in a way that heats every nerve ending along my skin.

I do not find his presence frightening now, but more... exciting. I am in awe of his strength and silence, and I want to know more about him. I want him to talk more freely to me, but I think that can only come with time and obedience.

My heartbeat quickens as I look at the flowers in the row, carefully keeping my eyes away from where I heard the footsteps. They move toward me, giving me the warning I need to keep my eyes averted. It is not fear I feel as the beast moves closer, but anticipation. I *want* him to be closer. I want him to touch me, maybe even kiss me. I want him to lose control with me the way he did before, but now he seems more determined to maintain a bit of distance.

I bend to smell a flower but do not turn. I know I'm not allowed to. The scent of the flower is rich, and I do not think I've ever smelled one like this before. It would make a lovely perfume. I inhale once again.

"I have been thinking," he says, his low voice rumbling through the terrarium.

I straighten up, my face hot and my heart fluttering. His scent is in the air now, and it is more noticeable to me than the aroma of the flowers.

"Yes?" I say, trying to keep my voice light.

I walk down the row, feeling him move with me and resisting a strong urge to turn and see his face. He feels human when we are together, and I want to know what he looks like, but I have to obey him. He feels like...I do not wish to think of that.

"You can write a note," he says. "And I'll ask the magic if it will deliver it."

A note?

"To my father?" I dare to breathe and before I can regret the clarification he breathes, "yes."

I stop, blinking hard as tears come to my eyes. I did not expect him to let me do this. I thought it would only come after many years of proving myself to him.

"I thought," I begin, my throat dry. "I thought the magic was only at the gate. I thought it was only here with you, at the castle."

"Do not underestimate what magic can do," the beast answers, and did I imagine it or is there a hint of amusement in his voice?

"How do you know if the magic will deliver the note?"

"There is no way of knowing," he answers, and then a piece of paper and a pen float over to me.

I did not expect to write to my father today, but I have thought about what I might say. The choices seemed endless at first. There was too much to tell him about. But now, after so many days of thought, I know that the best thing to do is to keep my message simple.

It *is* simple. I cannot leave and staying here will keep my father safe. I only want for him to find a bit of comfort in the note.

Father, I write. *I am safe. I am somewhere you cannot find me or fight for me, and I do not wish for you to do that. Please know that I am well. If I can send comfort I will do everything in my power to get it to you.*

All my love, Elle.

As soon as I finish, the letter floats out of my hands. I do not follow its path, because I know where it will be going—back to the beast, and I can't look at him.

"I will offer this to the magic," he says.

"Thank you." I breathe, suddenly overwhelmed by the emotion of being allowed even this small chance at contact with my father. I take a few moments to steady myself. "Will you walk with me?" I ask.

The beast does not answer, and when I move again, his footsteps do not follow. He is gone again.

CHAPTER 19

THE PRINCE AND THE BEAST

Elle does not know how she looks when she is standing in the sunlight. I am certain of this, because she stood before me in the terrarium, blushing, with her heart beating quickly as if I was the interesting creature there. I was not. She was ethereal and as I watched her, I had to hold myself very straight and still so that I could concentrate on controlling the beast. He loved the look of her among the flowers, which were blooming in a colorful show, and wanted to lay her down in the garden beds.

It took a great deal of effort to stay in place while she wrote, and I couldn't help staring at the light shining in her hair and the curve of her neck beneath where she had tied her curls back with a ribbon that matched her dress. The dress itself was difficult to look away from, as the pink shade highlighted the color in her cheeks. She looked like one of the blooms had come to life, far more beautiful than it had been when it was a flower.

I'm enraptured by the memory of her thoughtful expression as she wrote to her father and how she moved her pen carefully across the page, every word graceful. Fuck, she's gorgeous in all that she does. Tempting and naive. She has hope where I do not.

After our encounter in the terrarium, it's torture to wait for the sun to set. It is well within my power to seek Elle out during the day as she has asked me to. She proved yet again in the terrarium that she is capable of obedience even when she is not blindfolded.

But if I went to her, I would not be able to stop myself from touching her. I want my fingers in her hair and my hands underneath her clothes. I want her back in the light of the terrarium where I can see every inch of her skin exposed to the sun. If I did not blindfold Elle, I would truly be able to see all of her, uninterrupted by the line of black silk.

I want that too much to trust myself with the risk. All it would take is one flutter of her eyelids in the throes of passion and she would look upon me.

Several times, I stand still in my rooms and allow myself to sense her presence in the castle. It is always here, as Elle is forbidden to leave, but she moves around the halls, peeking into different rooms and always avoiding the tower...as she should. I wonder if she feels differently about her obedience today, now that I've allowed her to write to her father.

I cannot guarantee that he will read it. I cannot guarantee that the magic will take it to where it's bidden. That is outside my power.

But she was able to write it, at least, and that must feel like a reward for her beautiful obedience. A gift from me to her. Often in the day, she speaks to the magic, discussing her father. I know she loves him, and I have hurt her by taking her from him. The note is an offering of peace between us. A reward to her even.

It felt like a reward for me as well, though I know I am the least deserving of any kind of reward. Compared to Elle, I am nothing but a beast who has done beastly things to her and if I am honest, I have not regretted it. I do not know if I would be capable of regretting her presence in the castle. If I did, I think the beast might take over entirely and remind me of how sweet the victory is when the prize is a woman like Elle. Her sweet scent...and her moans of pleasure.

I shake my head and imagine, as my cock hardens, what I might be interrupting if I went to her now. She might be seated in a chair before the fire in the library, a book in her lap and a cup of tea on the table by her side. She might be in the kitchen, watching a recipe being prepared before her eyes by magic.

She is not bent over a chair with her hand between her legs, thinking of me biting into her soft flesh, hiding soft moans because she is so desperate for me.

Is she?

The sun takes an eternity to sink below the horizon. Finally, when the country is hidden in shadows and the sconces on the walls of my room have burned to life, I bathe, letting the hot water soothe the ache of all my pent-up energy. I dress, knowing that Elle will not see the items I'm wearing. I allow myself a few small comforts in the clothes I wear, as there is no one else but Elle and even she will not lay eyes on what covers my body. As I dress, I'm reminded of my image. *Nothing but a beast.*

My feet carry me down the halls to the room where she sleeps almost without thought. The objects that decorate the walls and alcoves might once have meant something to me, but they are only objects now. Once they bestowed wealth and elegance and grandeur. Now they represent the regretful past. The only thing that makes me care about them is that Elle has spent time in the castle, coming to know it as her home, and so she must have seen them, too. It is only the act of her taking any amount of joy in the decorations that gives them value.

I stop outside her door and knock.

The beast idly wishes to burst through the door, perhaps

even tear it off the hinges, and leave it in splinters so that no door can ever separate the two of us again. Elle takes a quick breath on the other side of the door.

"Yes?"

I imagine for a few moments that I have caught her in the heat of lust, thinking of me, but push the thought from my head.

"Put the blindfold on," I order. I intend to command her, but the words come out softer than I meant for them to. Almost as if in invitation.

There is quiet rustling on the other side of the door. With the beast's senses, I can tell that she is climbing out of the bed. Her footsteps cross to where the wardrobe is. The door opens, then closes. Does she keep the blindfold hanging up next to her hair ribbons? Is it front and center when she is not in her room, an essential part of her outside. Her footsteps move away from the wardrobe and the door.

"It's in place," she calls, her sweet voice causing my cock to harden even more. In some ways, it's unbearable to have Elle in my home, and this is one of those ways. Forcing myself to wait because she cannot be allowed to see me. What little trust we have built would be broken. And I enjoy her very much obedient.

I steady myself, giving her another moment to prepare, then open the door. I enter the room to find Elle standing in a long white nightgown in the middle of the floor, her feet bare and her hair spilling over her shoulders. My cock twitches at the sight of the firelight in her hair, bringing to mind how she looked in the terrarium earlier today. It was only hours ago, but it feels as if I've waited forever for this moment.

Now the black blindfold shines in the firelight, covering her eyes. I move at a restrained pace across the room and put my hand to her neck, feeling the thrum of her pulse beneath her skin and the rhythm of her breath. Elle instantly tips her face up to mine, her full lips parted and a pretty blush in her cheeks. Her pulse quickens under my palm. Elle trembles, but she does not reach for me. She obediently keeps her hands at her sides until I lower my face to hers and kiss her.

It is more controlled than the kiss we shared in the dining room, but it is no less deep. I mean to taste her without the beast pushing his way forward and taking over, though I cannot keep him down fully when she tastes so sweet, and her mouth is so soft and pliant and submissive for me.

The kiss deepens and Elle gasps, reaching for me and taking my shirt in her hands. She holds on as I lick into her mouth, thread my fingers through her hair, and tilt her head back to the angle I want. She sighs into my mouth, and I feel her wanting thick between us. As I kiss her, the tension grows, Elle's hands roam over my chest, and finally I pick her up in my arms and take her to the bed.

Elle arches her back as I lower her to the comforter, begging with her body to be touched. I kiss her there, too, and suck at the side of her neck, dotting her skin with shallow bites. I don't need to mark her here as well. I just want to remind her of how it feels to be bitten, and from Elle's gasps and moans, she hasn't forgotten. *It was everything to me. Something that must be done.* Her hips move underneath me, and she makes more contact through her nightgown. I slide one hand under it to one of her thighs and push it up to her waist, exposing her legs and her nakedness underneath.

Now the beast demands more. At the sight of her pink cunt peeking between her spread thighs, he lets out a growl and shoves until he has enough control to use my tongue and lick her. He breathes her in, sensing how the scent of her has filled the air around the bed, and my cock twitches. The beast ruts against the side of the mattress to alleviate some of the pressure building there, but it cannot be relieved without taking her.

I keep a tight hold on myself as Elle spreads her legs farther and her nightgown slips another inch toward her waist. I push both hands underneath, over her soft, delicate skin, and remove the nightgown, her hair slipping through it last. She makes a small noise at the feeling of air on her skin and lies back on the bed, more beautiful than any painting I have ever seen. More beautiful than any woman I have ever imagined. I kiss back down her body, lavishing my attentions on each nipple in turn, then leaving a wet trail down to her hips.

Elle pants softly, whining for more as I reach the softness

of her stomach and below to her thighs. The beast takes full control, overpowering me for a few moments, and he sinks my teeth into her thigh.

"*Oh*," Elle cries, and I bite her again a few inches from the first mark. The next sound out of her mouth is a deep moan. She is hot and responsive, beginning to writhe, and I have to pin her hips to the bed so I can devour her.

This time it's no small lick of my tongue over her center. I suckle all of her, tasting every inch of her cunt and sucking at her clit until she comes with a scream. Her hands clench wildly in my hair, and it only fuels me to enjoy her more and more. Elle moans, swept away by the pleasure, as I focus my tongue on her clit once more and bring her to a second orgasm that spills sweet arousal all over my tongue.

With her panting and sated, I can no longer ignore my own needs. I shove my trousers down, freeing my cock, and crawl on top of her, bracing my elbows next to her head. I drag the crown of my cock through her folds and find her entrance, then push myself in.

Fucking hell. I groan my pleasure into the crook of her neck. *She is the definition of heaven.*

Elle gasps and tilts her hips on the mattress as her body stretches to take all of me in. I fuck her with hard strokes, more beast than man, and Elle clings to me, trying to take me even deeper. It does not take long before she's coming again, her hot pussy clenching hard around me. It's my undoing. My pleasure spills out of me with a roar, blending in with Elle's cries. I push myself deep inside her and slip a hand between us, searching out her clit and bringing her to another peak while I'm still inside her.

Elle drops her head back against the comforter after and I take my time planting small kisses along her skin as her heartbeat slowly calms. I'm careful with her as I gather my composure and clean up the mess we've made. It's silent and I realize after a few moments that she has fallen asleep, no longer able to remain awake.

I sit back on my heels and watch her as she sleeps. Contemplating what she's done to me. And the hold she has over me. Pink marks rise on her skin from where I kissed and bit her. Her chest is flushed. She looks thoroughly fucked, and the beast growls his appreciation, and I feel his need to protect her.

Elle doesn't stir when I get off the bed and get a cloth with warm water to clean her better, and she is limp when I maneuver her to the pillows and pull the covers over her naked body. She appears so deeply asleep that I dare to undo the knot of her blindfold and leave it on the pillow next to her.

In the hallway, I close her door behind me. The air is fresh in the hallway as if the castle has opened windows to let a breeze in. It cools my skin as I walk, passing my own bed chambers and going to the tower. Elle's note has been in my pocket since she finished it at the terrarium.

On the highest floor of the tower, I open the stained glass window near where the rose sits silently in its cloche and look down. There is little to see in the dark, but the beast's senses can make out the grass below, the wall, and the forest.

I hold out the note and let it fall.

It tumbles through the air, and for a moment I think it will land on the grass. If it does, the rain and morning dew will turn it to mush and it will fade into the earth, never to be delivered or read by Elle's father. The thought offers me peace. I imagine it's what the magic will do.

At the last moment, just before I think it will hit the grass, the wind gusts, picking up the letter and carrying it away. It flies out over the wall and disappears.

It's only then that I second-guess the decision. But what's done is done. And one thing I know is that no one will take Elle away from me. Ever.

CHAPTER 20

ELLE

There are moments when I feel completely at peace in the beast's castle. I don't have a single worry or care, and it seems like nothing could disturb me. At times I am so content that I almost feel as if I've lived here forever and never known another life. It happens many times when I'm reading, lost in a story, my body warmed by the fire, drinking perfectly brewed tea, and in the back of my mind I can imagine having done this as a little girl in this castle and being loved and provided for without struggle. I imagine my mother not suffering like she did. Her with me still, and my father's heart never broken.

Of course, eventually I resurface from the story and that

vision disappears, and it suddenly seems odd to feel like I belong here. There's a great loss that I cannot avoid.

Although he fills it. *The beast.*

It shouldn't have happened so fast, should it? I know it has been weeks since I first arrived at the beast's castle, but that is not such a long time when you're a captive. And I *am* a captive. I cannot walk out the doors of the castle and go to the village and talk to my father. I'm not allowed to leave, and that means I don't belong. I wasn't born to the castle, and I didn't agree to marry the beast. I was stolen from my father's house and brought here without warning.

And yet I can't say that I've been hurt. I can't say that I've been treated poorly. I've been given a life I didn't know could exist in my wildest fantasies. And with that, comes guilt. And loneliness, apart from the fantasies I read throughout the day.

I look up from the book I'm reading, my eyes tired. I must've been reading for hours and hardly noticed the time passing. I've noticed the days have stretched easily like this. With peace and ease and entrenched in books. I would never have been able to lose myself in a story like this when I lived with my father. There was always work to do at the bakery or wood to gather for the fire or floors to scrub at the cottage. There was shopping to do and a tiny amount of money to count and stretch as far as it would go. There were meals to prepare, using as few ingredients as I could at a time to make it last a few more days. I could not have sat down and read until the only thing stopping me was that I needed a break for my eyes. Even if I had the light to read in bed, I would fall asleep, exhausted, before I could immerse myself in a book. But candles are hard to come by in the village and quite expensive. They're a luxury. So this...all of this? I refuse to take it for granted.

Reading was something I did only as a girl when my mother was alive. Back then, it seemed there was more time in the day and more things to do for pleasure. I know part of that was simply being a child and not knowing how harsh the world could be.

Although part of it was that I could not imagine a life of luxury like the one I live in the beast's castle. The beast stole me from a life of hunger and cold and uncertainty, and now I am reading in front of the fire in a dress finer than any my mother ever owned with slippers waiting on the rug to put my feet into that are likely more expensive than anything she owned, either. They're exactly my size, and they haven't been worn down by walking down the rough street in all kinds of weather.

This is the only time in my life when I have not wanted for anything. There aren't even rough underclothes in my wardrobe, nothing that would irritate my skin. If I think about wanting a bite to eat, a tray floats through the door.

I try to focus on the book in my lap, but my thoughts wander to the beast.

He is here, because he does not leave the castle. But I've still yet to see him and I've barely gotten to know him. It doesn't take much to feel his brokenness though. His need for love.

I frown down at the book. I have not gotten to spend as much time getting to know the beast as I would have liked, having lived in this castle for weeks. However, he does not seem like the kind of person—kind of beast?—who would kill for the love of killing.

If that's what he was like, then I would likely not be alive right now.

My chest aches, thinking about the beast alone here in the castle, which reminds me that my father is alone in the cottage. The magic gathers close to me and tries to soothe me as it senses my thoughts lingering on my father. I wish I could shove it all away. I do not wish to be soothed, I wish for answers. I wish to send this luxury to others. It feels selfish to have it all to myself.

I hope the magic delivered my letter. I hope my father is not trying to look for me. Worried out of his mind for my wellbeing. I can only imagine how angry and betrayed the beast would feel if my father came to the gates of the castle and refused to leave.

No one can know you are here.

Would he truly hurt the only other person I love? Oh, the thought comes quickly, and I choose not to think much of it and instead focus on the beast's command. I remember how the beast's voice sounded when he said those words to me. *No one can know you are here.* I understood his seriousness down to the core of me. That is why I told him that I did not need to tell my father where I was.

But I still pray the magic delivered the letter as he said it would.

I let out a sigh. Should I have pushed the beast to tell me why my presence here needed to remain a secret?

The magic answers for me. *No.*

My thoughts stray back to my father, who had been so heartbroken when my mother died. I know he won't fully recover from losing me as well.

For the first time, I'm beginning to think about what would happen if something were to happen to the beast.

It's an unsettling thought and brings on a surge of strong emotions. Why would I wonder that? Would *my* heart be broken? I feel things for him, of course. I feel drawn to him and intrigued by him, and I find myself missing him when I have run out of things to do in the castle and want someone to talk to. I am lonely without him. I love what he does to me and how I crave him more than anything else within the confines of the castle.

Am I...falling for him?

"I want to make tea," I say quietly. "I'd like to make it myself."

The tray floats into the room a few minutes later and

the tea things spread themselves out on the table next to my reading chair in the bedroom. There is enough room for the kettle and the pot, along with two cups. The first time I asked for this, the house brought me tea. I did not know what to do with the magic then. I don't know if this counts as *doing magic.*

What I know is that when I touch the kettle, the water inside begins to heat. It's not an instant process and it takes a few minutes before it whistles. By then I have prepared the leaves. I take the kettle and pour the water over them. I breathe deeply, clearing my head while the leaves steep, and then I touch the pot.

It pours a perfectly portioned cup of tea into one of the cups, then settles back on the table.

I add milk and sugar to the tea, then lift the cup from the table, imagining as I do that the cup and its matching saucer could talk.

If they could, I would talk to them.

I would talk to anyone or anything who would listen and converse at this point.

Emotions fill my chest again, but this time it's a sorrowful loneliness. I'm so lonely that I would talk to a teacup. All the fine things in the world can't replace a person who listens to you and tells you their ideas.

I laugh a little, though it sounds almost like crying. Have I gone mad? Is this what it's like to go mad? My loneliness twists at my heart, getting deeper as I sip at the tea. It is hot, but not so hot it burns my lips. The perfect temperature.

Can I complain about loneliness when I am lonely in such luxury?

I try not to think about it, returning to the peace of my book.

I have managed to sink into the story when there are footsteps at my bed chamber door.

It's him. My body heats instantly. I know it is. The moment he walks through the door, the room fills with his masculine presence.

I do not turn my head toward the door, but I put a finger in my book and close it, my breath coming faster. As I decide what to say, the silence isn't comfortable. It's not entirely uncomfortable either.

"How are you this morning?" I ask the beast, bracing myself to hear only silence. Maybe he will not want to tell me.

"I am well," he answers, a slight tension in his voice, but no outright unhappiness that I can hear. I want to ask him, *are you happy?* I want to say *is this what you were hoping for when you took me?* But the words refuse to leave my throat.

I open the book, make a mental note of the page number, and set it aside on the table.

"Will you ever let me see you?" I keep my voice soft, but my chest aches. I don't want to challenge him. I simply want to know.

This time, there is much more tension in the room and

the silence before he speaks is longer.

"Do you have your blindfold with you?"

"Yes," I say, exhaling.

"Put it on."

I get it out of my pocket and tie it around my eyes with shaking fingers. Then I sit up straight and fold my hands in my lap. He has not said to get up, so I don't.

The beast's footsteps get closer. I listen intently for each one, my heart beating harder as he crosses the room to me. Then his large hands—they feel *so* human and strong—are on my face, tilting my head.

His mouth crashes against mine as if he spent all night thinking of this and couldn't wait another second. Was this the tension I heard in his voice? The kiss feels needy. The beast wanted someone, and the person he wanted was me.

The lust and headiness is as unexpected as it is divine.

I open my mouth and let him kiss me even deeper as he slips a hand under the hem of my dress and finds my warmth between my legs, pushing aside my underthings to stroke me, and I cannot resist the sounds of pleasure that slip from my lips. My core heats and desire spreads over every inch of my skin with a vengeance.

The beast kisses me until I'm dizzy with the sensation, and then he pulls me upright and turns me around, guiding me back to my knees onto the chair. Both his hands move to my hips, and he tugs down my underthings, pulling them all the way off over my ankles, and then he braces my hands on the tall back of the chair. I feel small in it, almost like prey caught by a predator, and then the beast kisses the side of my neck and lets out a low sound.

I love this. I love what he does to me.

"Yes." I breathe, not knowing what I'm answering. I fall into his presence even faster than I would fall into a story. He is hard behind me, and there is the sound of cloth as he undoes his trousers and takes himself out.

The beast turns my head to the side and kisses my mouth hungrily again, and I kiss him back. One of his hands moves to my hip and tugs them backward until I am in the position he wants.

"Please," I beg him. For more. I need more of him.

And then his length is pressing against my opening, hard and hot, as if he owns me. I accept with a moan. It is the utmost pleasure to be filled by him. My body melts around the beast as he begins to fuck me with deep strokes.

My hands grip the edge of the chair. Holding on for dear life.

I would let him fuck me forever if his mouth moved between my mouth and my neck the way he's doing now, growling against my skin and licking and sucking and tasting. He can take me whenever he desires.

If he would only keep doing that, I would ask him to stay in my bed through the night. I would keep the blindfold on all night, sleeping in it, if that's what he needed.

I do not realize I've said any of those thoughts out loud until the beast releases a growl that sounds as if he is pained by hearing me say it. I think it's a warning, too, so I hush, but my silence is quickly broken by another moan as he finds my clit with his fingers and rubs, working me to a fast, hot orgasm.

The aftershocks make my mind hazy, and as it finally begins to clear, he lifts me off the chair and puts me on my knees on the rug. It's very plush and warm from the fire. The beast's hands on my face are warm. He brushes his thumb over my bottom lip and I open my mouth for him, not caring if I seem wanton or greedy. I've been alone too long and I want every bit of company I can get.

I want *his* company. I don't daydream about talking to anyone else.

His thumb is replaced by something else. A blush heats my cheeks as I realize. I take his cock in my mouth, tasting the two of us mixed together and relishing his muffled groans as I suck. The beast comes with a jerk of his hips and a groan. I swallow his release, salty and thick, and he comes down afterward slowly, one hand on my face and the other in my hair.

My heart races and with the blindfold on, all I can do is wait. All I can think in the silence after a moment is *please don't leave me*. It's not what I say though. I ask him for the one thing that makes me crazed with need.

"Will you ever let me see you?" I whisper. I'm falling for him. Madly and deeply and yet I still haven't seen him. I have no idea of what the beast looks like.

He strokes his fingers down my cheek, then takes his hands away.

I do not hear him leave the room, but the silence goes on for a long time.

When I finally gather my courage and lift the blindfold, he's gone. And my heart is shattered.

CHAPTER 21

THE PRINCE AND THE BEAST

Elle cannot know how it tears me apart to stay away from her. She has no idea how it tortures me not to be inside her every minute of the day. It's even beginning to torture me that she can't see me. She can't truly know me. Or who I used to be. The pain grows with each passing day that I realize she'll never know the man I used to be. The prince who she could have stood proud next to.

She could never love the beast I've become. If only I could go back to what once was.

I thought it would be easy to go without being known, but perhaps I only convinced myself of that after all those long years in the castle. Perhaps I only told myself I did not need to be seen and known because I know too well how it is when people see and judge *without* knowing.

When I leave Elle, I do it with my hand over my heart and a strange emotion in my chest. I think it is longing, but I thought I was past longing for things many years ago. I thought I had come to terms with the bargain I'd made.

All those lives for mine. That was what I did. I accepted this isolation in exchange for saving the village, my most loyal men, and the innocents I was supposed to protect. I thought then that there was a chance of ending the curse, but after I knew there wasn't one...

I go back into my rooms, the door closing quietly behind me, holding in pain and anger and most of all, regret.

I want to go back to her. *Why do I want what I cannot have?*

"I cannot have it," I yell to the windows in my room, pacing in front of them, purposefully not looking too far past the wall. The rage rises from the beast as I pace. There are many things I could have done in those lands if I hadn't accepted the witch's bargain, but that would have meant sacrificing the innocent, and I couldn't do that. That's not the duty of a prince.

A prince has to protect his people. It was my duty...but then it all changed, and I never knew that was a part of the deal.

"Why do I *want* this?" I growl, hearing the beast in my voice.

"I don't want her to see me," I say, and then I say it again. I say it until I almost believe it.

And I have many reasons to believe it. If Elle sees me for what I truly am, she'll never want me to touch her again. I've looked upon the mirror many times years ago. I've seen the hideousness and terror of the beast. A prince no longer exists. Even when I look upon my flesh, I know it is not what is seen.

I pace around my rooms until I've exhausted the urge to run and the beast has settled. He must sense that I'm not going to go back to our Elle.

It feels like days instead of hours when the large tray from the kitchen follows me to Elle's room. I do not know as much about her as I want, but what I know is that she loves being fed delicacies. She did not have enough food when she lived in the village, and I can give her this. I will remind her of what I provide and be thankful for that.

This time, when I knock, there is only a short pause, and then she calls, "I've put my blindfold on."

I go into her room. "I've brought dinner for you, my beauty."

Elle's smile and blush that come with it make the hours of waiting worth it.

I feed Elle from my hand on the rug before her fireplace, the two of us seated on comfortable cushions the house has provided. Elle hardly stops smiling. I feed her a sweet bite, then a savory one.

She enjoys my company; I'm sure of it. That pleases a piece of me that's desperate for her love. I want her to crave every bit of me that she can. I want her to need me so that if the day comes where she sees me, she will stay. She must. I do not know what I will do if she cannot find it in herself to…

"It's all delicious." She sighs after pulling her lips away from my fingers. The slight suction reminds me of the pleasure she provided earlier. I fucking love it. "Every bite."

"Then why are you making it harder to feed you?"

Her mouth drops open. "Am I?"

"I can hardly fit this bite between your lips."

Elle opens her mouth wider, her cheeks pink underneath the blindfold.

"That is better." I grin wickedly, enjoying the sight of her before me. I tease her and feed her and relish the moment.

The more she eats, the more relaxed I feel. The more relaxed Elle feels as well, or at least the magic in the castle is warming to this. My heart pounds with feeling. I did not intend to let any emotion I feel about Elle become so strong, but how could I prevent this?

She has come into the castle that has been my prison for so long and treated it like a home. She has awakened the magic in all the rooms, even the ones I allowed to become the most forgotten. The halls that used to be occupied with life and celebration have come back to life, although they are vacant when I pass…unless she is there.

I stroke the side of her cheek, and she smiles at my touch. Brightening and leaning into me.

It is late when I banish the tray, sending it back to the

kitchen for the dishes to be cleaned and put away for the night. What I should do is get up and leave her to the rest of her evening, but my eye catches on something sitting on a table near the chair by the fireplace in her room.

"What have you been reading?"

Confusion crosses Elle's face, but then it is replaced with excitement. I wish I could see her eyes. I can't, as they are covered by the blindfold.

"Oh," she begins, sounding delighted. "A book about a man who sails across the sea and has many different adventures when he arrives." Elle smiles. "I find them thrilling."

It has been years since I have read but I vaguely remember the tales of adventure. The memories bring back much emotion, but I suppress it, instead focusing on her gorgeous face.

"Read to me," I request before I can help myself.

Her shock lasts longer. "*Read* to you?" she asks.

"Yes."

I turn her around on the cushion, facing her toward the fire, then retrieve her book and rearrange my own cushion so I am seated behind her. I place the book in her hands, then touch the knot at the back of the blindfold.

"You will not turn around, my beauty," I murmur as I tap the knot of the blindfold.

"I will not turn around...I promise," she whispers in agreement.

Then I take the blindfold off.

She flips through the book, her head bowed, perhaps finding another place to start. I think she is scanning through the words because she lifts her head and starts to turn to look at me, inhaling as if she's going to speak.

I'm halfway out of my seat before I can see her eyes. Elle jerks her head forward, and I freeze, waiting to make sure she won't turn around again before I settle onto the cushion.

"I'm sorry," she says. "I'm so sorry. I'm just...are you sure you want me to read to you?"

"I would love for you to."

She smiles, and though I can't see her face, I can see it in her body and the ease that she settles into.

Then Elle tells me she's just got to a place in the book that would be perfect and asks if it's all right or if I'd like to start at the beginning.

The tale is a thrilling one and the cadence of her voice is entrancing as she reads to me. I think she has returned to a part she has read before, because the words fall smoothly from her lips. It is all so beautiful that I am lulled into relaxing. Slowly, she rests against me and her touch and her voice... they are everything.

It has been so long since I allowed myself to enjoy the leisure that life has to offer. I've spent my days wanting to go back in time. It has been so long since pleasure was something I could have at all. Even surrounded in all of this. I had forgotten the pleasure of a beautiful voice reading an intriguing story.

As her cadence becomes more and more comfortable, I realize I'm genuinely interested in the hero and his travels, as well as Elle and the warmth of the fire. I catch myself closing my eyes for longer and longer periods of time. Once, my chin nods toward my chest and I do not know how long it stays there before I notice and lift my head.

The next time my eyes close, I concentrate on her voice until I can see the hero and his ship sailing across the waves in the sun. It's only after quite some time that I understand I've begun to dream, and shortly after that I realize that Elle has stopped reading.

I jerk my head upright and my eyes fly open. The angle of Elle's face says that she is about to peek over her shoulder. I shoot my hand forward and grasp her chin, turning her head toward the fire.

Elle trembles slightly in my hold, a faint fear in the magic between us. The fear is so slight that I realize she is also aroused by my touch, though I may have startled her by moving so quickly.

I cannot blame her for being tempted. Elle has been so obedient, but even she must wonder what I'm hiding from her. She might be tempted even now.

But Elle doesn't put any pressure on my hand. She keeps her eyes forward, and I keep it there, forcing my breath to slow.

I could put her on the chair, or the bed, or even the cushion she's sitting on right now. I could take her roughly and put her to sleep once again like I did last night. The desire is there, but the fear of what she could have seen...

"It's time for sleep," I command her, not asking her. I am also commanding myself because the beast wants Elle as much as I do. He growls for her, almost whining to be able to mark her, but I do not let him.

"Will you stay?" she dares to ask.

"No." My answer is immediate.

Elle nods in understanding, and I want to go to my knees in front of her cushion and spread her thighs and lick her until she comes all over my tongue. I will never tire of tasting that sweetness, and from the way Elle smells, all warm with desire like she craves my touch, she would not mind if I did so.

But after nearly falling asleep in her presence, I do not know if I could maintain the kind of control I'd need to have if I took her again.

I need to hold onto this forever. If I lose her...surely I will lose myself.

If I did that, I might succumb to the urge to give in to her request to stay for the night. I know Elle would try to keep the blindfold on as she slept, but there is no guarantee it is possible, and then the worst might happen. Her eyes would go wide with horror and fear, and it would not be something

I could take back.

I do not want that to happen, I remind myself sternly. I never want her to see what the curse has done to me, because everything we have together in the castle now would be destroyed.

I allow myself a moment more of feeling her breath, and then I slip my hand away from her chin. I'm saddened as I get up from behind Elle, watching her to make sure she doesn't start to turn. She doesn't. She keeps her eyes on the book that rests in her hands, one finger tracing the pages.

Is she imagining reading to me again?

I imagine her voice reading me more of the story. I even imagine continuing every night until we reach the end, then choosing another book from the library together. I could not let her see me, but I could read her the titles and describe them to her.

Reluctantly, I go out into the hall and close the door behind me with a firm *click*.

My senses and the beast's are attuned to her, and I cannot bring myself to leave right away. Instead, I stand outside the door and listen.

I wait until I hear her pad across to the bathroom that adjoins her room, then pad back to her bed and get in. I hear the rustle of the covers as she climbs into bed and settles.

"I'm tired," she says, and I do not hear the candles go out, but I know they do.

The walk back to my room is lit with similar candles, but it feels darker without Elle.

When I am back in my room, I go to the window and look out. It is true that Elle is safer with me in another part of the castle because of the beast's urges.

I peer up at the sky, wishing times were different. The sky is dark except for the stars. There's a new moon tonight. The new moon...pitch black. The beast craves the full moon. He nearly howls for it.

CHAPTER 22

ELLE

The beast's castle is indeed a gilded cage for a prisoner such as me.

It nearly feels wrong to call it a cage when I have roamed far and wide inside it, exploring every place but the one tower I have been forbidden to enter. I've had fresh air brought in by the windows and the walls cleaned of their years of dust. I have had floors that seem like they haven't been walked on in years polished to a high shine, and as far as I can tell, there are no more dark corners begging for attention.

Of course, my father's house was much smaller than the castle. I'm not sure how many of my father's cottage could fit inside the beast's castle, but it must be at least a hundred, if not many more. This place is a village of its own. I could walk the halls for hours at a time, taking different paths and rarely passing the same room twice. I know, because I have done so, methodically moving from hall to hall, keeping a list on a scrap of paper in my pocket so that I knew where I had already gone to coax the castle back to its rightful state. I could make a lifelong project of cataloging the artwork here, or rearranging the books in the library, or redecorating any number of rooms or suites or hallways.

I could *change* the beast's castle, if I had the will. I do not think the magic would stop me. I think, in fact, that the magic would enjoy the fresh energy of a newly redecorated room, or a hallway that had been someone's sole focus for a week or a month or a year.

Thinking of spending years in the castle never fails to remind me that I cannot leave, which is what makes this place a prison. It appears to me to be a cage, no matter how much peace I feel here. No matter how blatant a prison this is. I can't bring myself to long for my old life in the village.

I argue with myself over and over as I move through this new, lonely life. A *gilded* cage is special because it is made from gold. It is luxurious. I cannot help that merely thinking the word *cage* brings to mind something dirty and rusted, and none of the castle is dirty anymore. It's not even dusty. I have given it as much of my attention as I could, though I am only one person and there are countless rooms. The space is lighter even as the weather gets colder. The castle brightens despite the sun setting earlier every day, because it knows that I prefer it to be brighter. Living with so much dark and gloom around me as the beast has done for these many years—that would be a cage.

The fact at the heart of everything is that I am not free to leave. If I leave, the beast will not guarantee that my father will remain unharmed.

If I owe the man who raised me anything, it must be his safety. It's true that he could not keep me entirely safe after my mother died. I know he feared the day that he let the cold sink too deeply into my bones, or a cold, hard winter left us without food. I was more than aware that he could not stand up against the world alone and could not protect me.

I wonder if that eats him up inside. By now, he must have realized that I'm not going to return. He must have come to understand that his only daughter is gone. I cannot return the daughter I used to be to my father, because I am no longer the same. I have seen the inside of the beast's castle and the magic that dwells there, and even if I *could* walk out the doors and go back to the village, I would never be able to forget it. I would long for the castle but mostly for the beast.

One thought does meddle at the back of my mind... What I can do is remove the burden of survival from his shoulders. I know how heavy a weight my own survival must have been, because he could not think beyond giving me to Crawe in order to absolve himself of it.

As I get ready for bed one night in my warm, cozy bedroom, I'm grateful for my fine nightdress, satisfied from dinner, and unconcerned about where tomorrow's meals will come from, I think about my father.

He is not so far away in the village, yet he might as well be on the other side of the world. Is he missing me tonight, or is he secretly relieved that he no longer has to account for putting food for me on the table? I know he was broken by grief when my mother died, but I do not know how he will ultimately react to my absence. Will he harden his heart and convince himself that I ran off to escape him? Does he weep thinking of me and hope that one day I will walk back into his cottage and take him in my arms?

I still love him, though his lack of strength is clearer to me now. I do not think my father would survive years of isolation, even in a castle.

"I hope you are well," I whisper to him. He cannot hear me, but perhaps the magic will take my well-wishes to him on the wind. "I hope you are safe. Have you read my letter?"

The beast hasn't mentioned the note I wrote in the terrarium, and I haven't asked him whether he thinks the magic was successful. I don't even know if he gave it to the magic, or how he did so. Some have called me naive over the years, but I think he *did* send it. I think he kept his word and at least tried to have the magic carry my note. I hope it arrived, and that my father heeded what I said.

"Don't come here," I whisper. "Don't try to find me. Just know that I am safe and that I love you."

I'm still thinking about it the next morning when I wake, stretching in the warmth of my bed before bathing and preparing for breakfast.

I wouldn't have had the freedom of this solitude if I had been forced to marry Crawe. He would have expected things of me, and men like him do not care for women's comfort or pleasure. I would likely not have been able to walk the halls and watch the castle liven up for the morning. Now that I have spent the time coming to know this place, even the beds in the farthest bedrooms make themselves with what seems like optimism, as if the castle might soon be filled with guests again.

I often wonder how magical that would be. There is a lounge my father would love if he were here. It smells of cigars and fine leather and has books of mechanics and history that speak to my father's soul. Our love of books had often bonded us. I can hardly bear to enter that room. It pains me with the thought of never getting to tell my father of the tales in the books or to ask him how his day was.

Just as quickly as the sadness comes, so does the reminder to be grateful.

Life within beast's castle is better than most lives I would have had before. It's a certainty that I would have struggled as a single woman had I lost my father as well, because the world is not kind to young women like me.

Is the beast kind to you? A voice in my head wonders. *He stole you and made you his captive.*

Yes. He is.

More than anything, I think about the evening the beast brought me dinner and fed me there on the rug. I think of that evening many, many times a day. He has not repeated it since, and maybe it is because he nearly fell asleep in my room, and I almost peeked at him to find out if he had.

Was it that mistake that made him more cautious and distant?

I hope not. I would like to read to him again. Perhaps I will ask him if he would like that as well the next time he comes to me.

Or perhaps I will try to send him a note and have the magic of the castle carry it to him. It probably would. The castle is quite kind as is the magic. Although if its intention is kind, why was it so cruel to the prince?

The thoughts I have about the beast are much more forgiving than they might have been. After all, he has given me pleasure and pain that my body craved. He has not kept me imprisoned without food or light or human comforts, though he could have.

I often read about such things in fairytales as a girl and wondered how I might feel if I were transported into a different world from my own. I thought I would be overwhelmed with joy no matter the circumstances, too awed by the novelty of everything to worry much about how I had gotten there.

I had read those stories less as I had to work more to keep us fed, but looking back, the tales were similar.

In all of them, tragedy began a tale of wonderment.

That evening, as the sun sets, I return to my room, having seen no sign of the beast. His presence is everywhere I roam in the castle, but I did not hear his footsteps today nor smell the scent of him that makes my skin flush.

Perhaps I will see him later. I pick at the hem of my dress hoping to see him. I miss him. I miss him greatly.

My room faces the front of the castle. From my window, I can see the castle wall and the gate, though I dismiss them both with only a glance. Something far closer and far more beautiful has caught my attention.

A climbing rose has grown through the wall of my bedroom.

As I watch, the climbing stem grows steadily into my bedroom, clinging to the wall. Buds pop out of the green. It grows farther, snaking around the bedroom. I trace my fingers along the vine-like stem. The buds are already beginning to open like they would in the beginning of summer, though it's not the right time for them yet. I stroke one of the smallest buds with my fingertip.

"There's no sunlight in here," I tell the flower softly. "Not the kind flowers usually search for. If you want that, you should try the terrarium."

Thorns pop from the vine as well. I avoid them as I continue tracing the plant.

Before long, it has circled over the vanity like a wreath. Pink roses bloom on the decorative circle, almost as if the rose and the castle knew I was thinking of putting something there. I hadn't decided what, because I didn't want to leave a bare spot somewhere else, but now I don't have to decide. This rose plant has gifted me something beautiful for that space on the wall.

The scent of fresh roses fills the room. I relish it twice as much as I would in summer, when roses are plentiful. How can I not? It is clearly a sign of beauty.

This is what it must mean for a cage to be gilded. Filled with fine art and books and food and clothes, with magical roses growing to please the eye.

I close my eyes, inhaling the fragrance deeply. Lulled by the magic and the scent of the roses and the safety of the brick walls all around me.

I'm deep in memories, breathing the scent of the roses and thinking of summer and gardens of sunlight, thinking of how even the warmest, most pleasant summer in the village would still have been difficult for me and my father. I compare the life I have now to the life I led then when a scream jerks me back to the present.

It's a terrible shriek and a cry that curdles my blood.

My eyes fly open, and I freeze for a moment. It is so

strange to hear another person's voice. My heart pounds and my body knows something is terribly wrong. It is not the beast screaming, is it? *No*, the sound came from *outside* the castle. A second scream startles me into action. I rush for the window and my heart stops.

No. My blood turns ice cold at the sight long in the distance.

For the first time since I arrived at the beast's castle, there are people at the gate in the big brick wall. I realize much too late that my absence in the village was noticed. I knew my father would know I was gone and that Ara would know when I did not come to the bakery, but I did not think a group of people would risk coming to the gate to search for me.

There are maybe a dozen people? It's hard to make out so far away and everything happens so quickly. I do not know *why* they would have done it, because I recognize some faces but not Ara's and not my father's. I look harder, though they are moving and their faces are unclear. I want to call to them to run. Go far away! After all I do not know if they are here for me or for some other foolish reason.

And then the small crowd at the gate parts, and I suddenly understand exactly why this is happening. One man makes his way closest to the gate and stares through at the castle, and I recognize that face with a shiver of horror and fear. It is Crawe.

I've never felt so much dread in my life.

CHAPTER 25

THE PRINCE AND THE BEAST

The beast roars inside me, the sound of his fury blocking out all other sounds. It's hot, a burning inferno as he forces himself to the front. The tinge of iron from blood fills my mouth. For a few breaths, that is all I can hear, the sound ringing in my ears and throat and escaping me. It feels like it's loud enough to fill the castle and warn off the intruders, but they do not leave the gate.

All I can think is that they will not take her. I'll kill them all. They knew better than to dare come to my gate.

The beast roars again. I am not certain if I'm making the same sound that floods my ears, but an ache in my throat tells me I might be. A small part of me does not want Elle to hear this and become afraid, but I cannot stop it.

The people at the gate do not have good intentions. Their hatred is palpable.

From the window I can see that there are at least six of them, perhaps eight. I do not want to take my eyes off them, but I do so I can storm through the halls and reach the front entrance of the castle.

I burst out into the cold night air with a roar. This time, I hear the sound echo off the wall and come back to me. It's not enough to make the people at the gate—the *attackers*—turn and run. The beast did not expect it to, but the parts of me that are still human hoped their fear of the beast would end this before it truly began.

But they are determined and do not flee back to the trees. Anger floods my veins. There's something in my castle they want, and it can't be anything other than Elle. My Elle. *Mine.* She is the most valuable thing. More precious than all the food in my stores or the gold in my treasury. I would not even care to replace most of the other things in the castle.

Elle cannot be replaced. She cannot even be compared. There is no one else like her in the world, and I will not lose her to the mob. They've already taken enough.

Possessiveness fuels me to blindly charge across the front entry with fury flooding my veins. I should have known they would come looking for her. I should have known they would realize her value only after she was gone. As I approach the gate, this is confirmed when a man steps up closest to the iron. His face is etched in arrogance and his teeth are bared as he screams for Elle. *He dares speak her name.*

It's Lord Crawe.

A darkness spreads through me, cracking my bones as I charge while another murderous growl tears out of my throat. This man dares to challenge me at the gates of my own home.

How did they know?

Something must have given her away. Given *me* away. Perhaps it was only that the paper was too fine to have been from some other country village. It was the plainest paper the castle had to offer, and there was no other mark on it. If this is because of Elle's note at all—

It can't be. It can't be. If the magic delivered the letter, then it was slipped under her father's door or sent in through a crack in an open window, not hovering outside waiting for him.

This is the magic's doing. I know it deep in my soul. It wants me to fight for her and I will do more than that.

The beast roars with unrestrained rage as we near the gate. Neither of us can forget the last time villagers came here with evil intent. I remember it so clearly, though the beast was in control then, doing all he could to get my body to safety. He could hardly growl as he killed, defending himself, trying to stay alive. He snarls now with the terrible pain of those memories and how he was chased and beaten and hated, marked for death even though he hadn't killed anyone and had only wanted the village's help.

His rage and determination overpower all the caution I could have given him. I am pushed to the back and the beast is in full control.

This is so needless. It doesn't have to be like this. Let me have my one peace. My one love. My Elle.

In a single breath of hauntingly cold air, the beast speeds toward the gate; the last few feet fall away as he runs with all the power of his corded muscled body. The beast's bloodlust surges as we reach the gate and let out a final earth-shattering roar. Two men try to climb the iron gate. They have succeeded in reaching the top and throw themselves over, landing on their feet in front of me.

That's not good enough. I need all of them, because once I start to kill, I will not stop.

Once the beast starts to kill, he will not stop.

They've brought torches burning into the night and swords and batons of steel, but the beast's vengeance is stronger than any weapon they could forge. I almost feel pity for the unwise souls until I see his face—Crawe.

Another roar escapes without my conscious consent, and the magic understands that I want to let them through the gate. I do not want to do this because I think they will run from me and get away from the castle. I do it because the gate is no longer protecting me. It is an obstacle between me and my task.

The gate slams open, causing some of the men on the other side to jump back in shock. They take a moment to gasp, but then they recover and charge at me, their weapons held high and flashing in the light of the torches.

For a single second, they must think they have the advantage. There are more of them, and I am only one beast. They do not understand the depth of his rage, or mine.

The beast obliterates them, tearing their flesh and barely responding to an ounce of their attack. They are nothing compared to what he is. What he's capable of. I taste nothing but blood. I hear nothing but screams. The pain of a sword is nothing. The agony of a club to the head is nothing. They are nothing but dead.

One by one, he sinks claws and teeth into their flesh, ripping and tearing until the men begin to fall. He bites, snapping his jaw to cut through flesh until he meets bone. Blood spills hotly over his face and hands. It smells like copper in the cold air, mixing with the scent of the iron gate, and soon the blood is all there is.

There is nothing but pure primal need when *we* lunge for them. Suddenly there does not seem to be any distance between us.

The men go down one by one. One of the torches swipes at me, close enough to singe my skin, but I hardly feel the heat. That is not the kind of wound that will force me to stop. I don't pause for an instant.

I tear out the throat of another man. I use my claws and the stick and my teeth again and again and again, watching only long enough to see that the men don't get back up.

Then, suddenly, it is only me and Crawe. A gasp is heard to my right and I turn to face the sight of a coward.

Lord Crawe looks at me with disgust and anger and disbelief. There is also fear in his eyes, though he would never admit it. I bare my teeth at him, and he lifts his sword high, gritting his teeth. He thinks he will get the chance to come at me with it and pin me down and shove it through my chest, but he won't.

When he takes his first step, I leap at him, snarling and growling and ready to end this battle once and for all.

By the time our bodies meet, Crawe has a knife in one hand and his sword held in the other. I sink my teeth into his forearm, and he drops the knife.

Crawe leaps back a few feet to gain space, wiping at his mouth and wincing. He gets both hands on the hilt of his sword. We circle each other for a few steps, but the beast's vision is red with anger and he has no time for this man's game.

He attacks with teeth again, and then we are there, tearing at every piece of him we can reach. When Crawe falls with a pitiful scream, the beast is still not satisfied.

Mine. Mine. She is mine.

Blood spreads in a pool around Crawe's body as his throat is clawed away. The beast lets out a triumphant roar. He has won. He has killed all the men who thought they could scale the wall and kill him like a mere animal. No light sparks in any of their eyes. They are all finished, the battle is over, and the yard is silent.

The air is even colder than it was. It smells of snow. I inhale hard, my breath visible in the air in front of me, and my blood is still hot. In the silence I can hear the wind in the forest and echoes of that long-ago fight that happened almost in this very spot.

But as I catch my breath, the realization hits that I don't feel victorious.

I don't feel like I won. I don't even feel like I gained anything, though the beast disagrees. I know that I have done this to protect Elle and to protect myself, but as I look at the bodies, another emotion sinks in.

It is shame.

It is a grievous sadness. I stand in the yard, surrounded by dead bodies, and I don't feel powerful. I don't feel like the blood that was spilled tonight has made things any better. They will come for her again. They won't stop until I'm dead.

For a moment, I miss the world that I once had when I was the prince and not the beast.

The thing that brings me the most sadness is that Elle would have loved that world. She would have been safe. My home used to be filled with dinners, dancing, conversations, and laugher. It was never this silent and angry. It was never this burden, always with the knowledge that someone else may come to kill me.

There's a crack in my chest, loud enough that it is audible. I hear it and I feel something breaking open inside me. Almost at the same time, a stick cracks behind me.

I turn, feeling the blood on my hands and face and soaked through my clothes. She stands in the yard, her hair blowing around her face and her skirt blowing about her legs.

Her eyes are wide, and she is not wearing her blindfold.

She stares, horrified, at the beaten and bitten bodies that lay around me in a blood-soaked circle, her mouth open in shock and her hands shaking at her sides. Her chest rises and falls far too quickly. Panic overwhelms her.

Before I can do anything, before I can even speak her name, her eyes snap to mine, and the terror in them grows.

CHAPTER 24

THE PRINCE AND THE BEAST

For a few beats of my heart, we stare at each other as the night wind blows between us. Everything slows and dims around me as I watch the reality of what I am set in for my Elle. My beauty does not belong in the hell that this scene has become. The blood on the ground grows into larger, darker pools, spreading between the bodies. None of them utter a sound. They are all dead, so they will not be making any sound, ever again.

For a moment, I almost manage to convince myself that Elle and I are frozen statues, and that the magic has stopped time so I can hide what I've done. As if it would protect me. Or rather her innocence in all of this.

Would she believe me if I told her I didn't feel the need to destroy anymore? I don't feel the urge to hurt or bite or tear at or beat anyone at all. She tames the beast inside of me. It whines for her love more than the desire for vengeance. The beast's rage has faded as quickly as it came when I saw the villagers by the gate. The chill of the night has blown all of it away, and my heartbeat has slowed. I know the danger has passed.

But not for Elle. The danger is standing right in front of her. My heart pounds as she looks at me. Even now, part of me cannot do anything but look back at her.

There's not enough moonlight for my human eyes alone to be so aware of the color of Elle's, but the beast's senses do not need more than the moon. All they need is a small amount of light, and that is all he has, now that the torches the men brought are extinguished on the ground. Only one of them still burns and the flame is quickly turning to nothing more than an ember. I'm very aware of the bodies and their weapons strewn on the frost-covered ground and the last of the torchlight going out, but I am more aware of Elle.

The breeze blows a lock of her hair across her face, and I feel rather than see the final torch extinguish.

That is what seems to break the spell cast over both of us.

Elle bolts away, and I am jolted out of the stillness of the moment and back into the pain of my disappointment and my regret and of all the frustration I have kept inside me since the witch's curse. It takes my body a few seconds to awaken again, giving her a small lead on me. I chase after her as she goes, her hair flying behind her and her skirts bunched in one hand.

Her attempts are futile. She is helpless in the face of what I am.

She tries to run through the gate, perhaps thinking she can run through the woods to the village. I let out a roar of despair and magic blows through the yard. The gate slams shut just before Elle reaches it. She turns on her heel, eyes wide and full of fear, and runs back toward me for a step before she cuts in another direction, parallel to the wall.

That pain and anger stir inside of me, the pain though... it's brutal. I knew this would happen.

The wall goes on for miles. She must know that she can't escape by finding an edge. She must know that I have told the magic I do not want her to leave, and she will find it difficult to climb any part of the wall now.

She has to know it won't be possible to escape, but she runs anyway. Heaving in air as tears stream down her face.

Another roar swells and dies in my throat as I chase after her. Letting her run. Letting her exhaust herself so when I catch her, the fight will be minimal.

This is my worst nightmare. I could not imagine a more terrible way for Elle to finally see me with her own eyes. There were things I could not hide from her, since she was my prisoner. I could not hide that I was willing to keep her prisoner. I could not hide that there were consequences she would not like if she were to flee.

But killing the villagers she undoubtedly knew was not how I wanted her to understand what I have become. Crawe, a man she spoke to...the others, I do not know who they are. A splinter flares in my chest. Her father perhaps? I do not know. I barely saw their faces.

She has seen the worst of me tonight. The part of me that did not hesitate to murder through any means necessary, with teeth and claws and beating the villagers with a stick until they fell. I pray her father was not among them. Fuck!

She is running for her life, and the beast knows it. This truth sharpens his senses, making his vision clearer than it had been. He doesn't fight for complete control, but his dominance over her rages inside of me. His need for her is everything. Some of his rage returns as Elle continues to run. He has claimed her more than once; she belongs to him. She should not flee for so long without stopping and sinking to the ground, showing him she understands her place here.

Elle runs with everything she has, and she is fast, but everything works against her. Her feet leave dark prints in the frost on the ground. If I wanted, I could stop chasing her and walk, and her footprints would lead me to her. Even if she went inside the house, it would take nothing for me to scent her, no matter where she attempted to hide. I could so easily hunt her down.

My mind is heavy with swirls of the memories and the magic and the needs of the beast. It's as if I'm losing my mind.

Elle tries to change directions and stumbles. The beast inside of me lunges at her, planning to pin her down, perhaps even bite her again to remind her that he claimed her many weeks ago and this attack by the villagers, and even her fear of the attack, does not change that. He wants to remind Elle that she belongs to him. That she belongs to *us*.

I will never be able to erase the memory of what happened from her mind. I want to tell her that it had to be done, both because the beast cannot be tamed and because men like that will not give up until they are dead. Men who believe they have some claim on another's life will not stop until their own lives are ended.

I could not let them take her away. I want her to understand that, and I do not know how to make her see that.

All that comes from my throat is another furious growl.

Elle steps out of my way and presses herself up against the wall, her back to the bricks. Her breath is ragged, and she squeezes her eyes closed as if she can pretend she never saw me.

With adrenaline pounding through my veins and every inch of my skin on fire, I cage her against the wall, trying to bring my face down to hers. I want to lick over her pulse and make her submit. To bite and hold her still.

But Elle turns away, facing the wall with her hands against it, her back to me, rejecting me as her cries grow stronger.

A sharp pain shatters what's left of the human side of me.

This was my greatest fear, and it has come to this. Elle, blocking me out as much as she can with her body, because she can't bear to look. Because she's now afraid of me and blames me for what happened tonight.

Elle will never forget now that she has seen the beast.

My body shakes with fear as I tower over her. Fear that I have lost her forever even though I'm far too aware I never deserved her to begin with. This was all a mistake. Unable to think straight, I leave her. Hating the beast, hating myself, hating the witch, and hating the villagers.

I'll find her again. She can't run from me forever.

CHAPTER 25

ELLE

Has the magic driven me mad?

I stare at the ceiling in my bedroom, my body exhausted and my bones seeming to ache with constant sadness.

Maybe I have gone mad, and now this is all my mind can do. Stare at the ceiling and wonder how it all went wrong.

"It was wrong from the beginning," I whisper to the ceiling. "I should have known it would always be wrong."

No matter how many times I ask the questions, the ceiling never answers and neither do the roses.

The roses are what might convince me that I am out of my mind.

"It was ruined from the beginning," I tell the ceiling and

the roses again.

But in my heart, I cannot believe that.

Is it the magic that makes me think it's not true? That there was something I had with the beast before he became brutal and merciless? The only thing that spares my heart is that my father was not among the men. But the very thought that he might come...my bottom lip wobbles and I have to find a way to beg the beast.

"The beast," I whisper. It's harder to stop talking to myself and to the roses. It's harder because I'm so tired, and I'm so sad, and sometimes it feels as though the better idea would be to pretend it never happened. Sometimes my mind tries to convince me it didn't happen. That it could have been a terrible dream, and now I am wide awake with the visions haunting me and my questions and prayers going unanswered.

I am so terrified and shaken I cannot even roll to my side. I can only stare at the ceiling of my bedroom. A tear drips down my face to my pillow, but I do not move.

I keep telling myself Crawe was a bad man. He needed to die. They would have killed the beast and for what? For me? It's hard to swallow with the guilt and shame.

And then I see his beastly face. An image of something I'd never imagined.

He is a beast, but when he touches me he is a human. I know it is so. The magic did not deceive me every time I felt his hands on my body or his body over mine or his lips on my skin. I *know* he is human when we touch.

But the beast I saw when Crawe came to the castle...

What *was* I seeing? I have no explanation for the things I remember. Perhaps the two are not the same. My mind plays tricks on me. So many of the beast's orders don't make sense, and I cannot tell if it's him or me who is mistaken.

I squeeze my eyes closed, trying to forget. I have tried to forget so many times, but it does not work. If for no other reason than to give sleep to my burning eyes and rid my mind of the sight of tonight. The memories are a permanent thing, unless the magic can offer me something to forget them.

I shake my head as if the magic had floated me some sort of potion to take away the memories. It hasn't. I think if the castle did have such a thing, I would have been offered it by now. But I do not want to forget, and neither does the castle.

I think, though I cannot be sure, that the castle does not know what to do, and so it is repeating the last thing it knew to bring me comfort and joy. It is filling my room with roses.

So many roses.

The wreath of roses above my vanity is no longer visible. It has been completely covered by more plants that have shoved themselves in through the opening that the first climbing rose peeped from. They grow along the walls of my bedroom in masses, their scent filling the room with a suffocating sweetness. It is harder to breathe in here almost every minute, but I don't have another choice, because finding another place to go would mean getting out of the bed, and I cannot do it.

By the time I get out of bed, with sleep evading me, I do not know what the magic will have done. Perhaps the roses will have filled the entire castle. If they keep growing at this rate, their thorns will cut into me as I lie here in the bed.

"Don't do that," I manage to say, louder. "Don't fill up the bedroom. I have to be able to breathe." The words come out numbly as more tears slip down my cheeks.

Somewhere in the castle, the beast is breathing too.

Thinking about tonight like I am, most likely. I was already outside when the first two villagers, who I recognized from my work at Ara's bakery, reached the top of the iron gate and jumped down. They were the first to die, because they were closest to the beast when he attacked.

The men's screams from that night fill my ears as if they are still happening. Their shrill shrieks send shivers down my spine. For so long, I listened to the tales of the beast and the castle and the magic. I listened to what happened to the villagers who tried to capture and crucify him. I heard stories of those screams, and I thought I had imagined them vividly. I used to have dreams about those stories when I was a girl and would wake up with tears in my eyes from imagining the howls of pain.

What I imagined was not like the reality. The screams of the dying men were more like wounded animals. Some of them didn't have time to scream. Some of them made worse sounds. It was as if it was all happening mere steps in front of me, though most of the killing was done when I stood at the front entrance, watching with horror and shock as the beast tore into those men.

The stories hadn't prepared me.

Either that, or I didn't listen carefully enough, because I told myself I was drawn to the beast. I told myself he couldn't be that kind of person from the lore. I told myself that the stories couldn't be true, because if they were, he would not treat me as he has...I could not feel for him as I do.

And yet I saw with my own eyes.

More roses bloom, the stems growing across the ceiling. Buds pop out of the vines and open until they are the size of two of my fists put together. I have never seen blooms so large. It's as if the magic is determined to impress me and thinks if it can only make the roses large enough, I will recover.

Does it not know that in my mind, my father and friends could have been massacred just the same? And I could do nothing but watch?

The roses that bloom above my head in brilliant shades of red only remind me of the blood that was spilled at the gate. There was so much of it. There seemed to be too much. I didn't know there could be that much blood in one man, let alone the group at the gates.

I can't stop seeing it. "Make it stop." I plead to the magic.

"Please," I whisper.

My chest aches. I miss my father now more than ever. While I lie in bed, desperate to think of anything else, I think of all the ways he had not been the perfect man. He had struggled to feed us. He had struggled to do anything after my mother died. We worried about keeping the cottage warm in the winter and about going hungry. We had many worries, but I never worried that he would run through the front door of the cottage and slaughter the people of the village. He would never harm a soul.

The pain grows until I'm crying at the thought of never seeing him again and if I do, it would be his death. It takes a great deal of energy, but I push myself upright on the pillows so I can breathe more easily. There is so much pain. There is only pain, and I cannot think of a way to ease it.

I did not see his face, but there was quite a distance between the front doors of the castle and the gate. It was dark, without much moon, and the torchlight flickered, making it hard to make out anyone's features clearly. I knew Crawe because I had thought about him often in the days when I thought I would have to marry him. I knew the men who climbed the gate because I saw them most days in the village, and one of them would come in to buy bread every three days, always on the same schedule.

As time goes on, my memory fades and I do not know anything for certain anymore.

There are times when I search my memories and think I caught a glimpse of my father when the gates flew open, and then I spend hours trying to decide one way or the other.

I cannot decide.

Is he safe now?

Or did he die at the hands of the beast? Am I forced to mourn him because I wished to send word that I was unharmed, and somehow he guessed where I was? It is the only place I truly could be isn't it? What a foolish girl I was.

At the front of the gate, where I stare for hours, nothing remains. There is no evidence of the horrors and that only makes it worse.

More guilt stabs into my chest. Is this all my fault? I did not think one note could possibly lead to this, otherwise I would never have sent it. I would have been heartbroken for my father, alone in the village and wondering where I had gone, but wouldn't it be better for him to be sad rather than dead?

The question that riddles most frequently in the lonely hours is *what can I do to fix this now?*

I slump down on the pillows, unable to stop crying and unable to think of any way out of this grief. It might not be necessary if my father is alive, but how will I ever find out?

I cannot leave. The beast will not let me.

And the feelings I have about this are strange and growing stranger. They are growing too strong to deny, and I cannot reconcile what happened that night with the emotions that grip me at all hours of the day and night.

More flowers bloom over my head, turning the gilded cage into a prison of red.

THE PRINCE AND THE BEAST

I pace the halls as I've done the past three days. This is not what I wanted when I ran to the gate to defend my home and the woman inside.

I did not want her choking on the perfume of roses filling her room. I did not want her too disturbed to rise from her bed. I did not want her to loathe or fear me.

The beast growls, feeling her despair even as he watches her through the mirror, through my eyes.

I have not gone to her room since the night the villagers attacked. The beast does not like this. He wants to intervene, to bring her back out into the castle, which is already feeling her absence. The dust is not yet collecting in the places it once was, but on the rare occasion I leave the mirror and walk the halls, they are growing more shadowed.

The magic echoes her agony, and I do not know how to stop it.

I only know how to share in her hate for what I've become and what I've done.

CHAPTER 26

THE PRINCE AND THE BEAST

I've lost count of the number of days it has been when I finally break.

It has been my habit to let Elle determine the life she lives in the castle, so long as she stays obedient and does not try to leave. The first night I brought her here, I did go to bed with her. The beast had not been willing to accept anything else. He had been patient enough, carrying her through the woods without lying her down on the grass and having her then, and he could not be held at bay any longer.

In truth, neither could I. There had been too many years of solitude before Elle came through the gate in the wall and found the swing. I had not been able to touch a woman in so long, and from the first breath I took of the scent of her skin, I knew she was mine.

Every little detail of how we began consumes my waking thoughts. The details of how I lost her meet me when my eyes close and the terrors of that night return to haunt my dreams.

I made her mine, and that was no easy task. It was not easy to wait when I heard the words her father said to her. It was not easy to hang back, knowing that anything could happen to her in the village. It was not easy to have that patience, waiting until she was safe behind the castle walls to do what I wanted and what the beast demanded.

I waited, and I was rewarded with her submission.

Yes, she was afraid, and she was wary of me, but what did I give her other than pleasure? Surely I made up for her fear. Surely I did not turn out to be a fearsome creature of the night. It is I who brought her here and I who gave the magic my blessing to make her as comfortable as she can be.

And Elle cannot say she did not enjoy it. I saw her in the library all those many days. I know she delighted in having the kitchen prepare recipes for her. She was lighthearted, and as a result the castle became more serene as well.

I cannot watch her cry through the tarnished mirror in the tower for another moment.

I rise from my chair, the old wood creaking. The moment my eyes lose their focus on Elle, they land on my own reflection. After all these years I am used to the sight of the beast in the mirror, but I feel a disappointment that I did not think I would feel again. What did I expect? I am the beast, and nothing will change that. There is no hope of seeing my former self in the mirror again.

With a hopeless feeling I haven't known in so long, I'm at her rooms without remembering any of the journey. My feet have carried me here with the same urgency they carried me to the gate that night. This problem is one that must be attacked without any further wait, because the castle has done its best. It has brightened Elle's room with roses and sent her things to eat and opened her window as she cried, giving her fresh air until she shivered from the outdoor cold on her skin. It can do no more.

Elle cries on the other side of her bedroom door when I knock loudly, my heart beating fast.

"Put your blindfold on." I call through the door.

Elle does not answer. She only cries, her sobs becoming a bit softer. I do not hear the telltale creak of the bed as she reaches for the blindfold. I do not hear her agreement. Pain flows through my being.

"Please put the blindfold on." I try again, though I am certain she can hear the impatience in my voice. What she cannot hear is the agony her pain puts me through. I can bear it no longer.

"Elle," I call out and bang my fist against the door. "Answer me!"

She clears her throat while sniffling. "Why? When I have seen you for what you are?"

"For your comfort," I answer as calmly as I can.

There is a pause so long I think she has chosen to ignore me and my blood boils. The control I had over her is seemingly gone and I do not want to discover what that means for us.

Finally, she answers. "I do not wish it."

"Do it *now*," I thunder, losing what little control I had over my temper. My voice echoes in the hall and the castle seems to fall silent around me. That cannot be anything but an illusion brought on by the volume of my own voice after many hours of silence.

Elle sucks in a small gasp. "Will you harm me if I do not?"

I want to slam my fist into the door to release some of the frustration that burns within me, but I clench both my hands at my sides, breathing deeply. I can hear Elle's breathing on the other side of the door with the beast's senses. She inhales quickly, still crying but no doubt shocked by how this has come to an argument through a closed door.

"Will you harm me if I do not?"

The emotion at my chest feels so tight that after a few deep breaths, it becomes hard to continue. My corded muscles ache from holding myself back for so long.

"Why do you wish to torture me?" I ask her lowly through the door.

Elle lets out a sound that may be a laugh or it may only be

another sob. "It is I who is tortured. My mind is playing tricks on me. I wish to see you so that I may not lose what sanity I believe remains."

I know she is on the edge. I know she has been consumed by sadness and is at a loss for herself. But there is something else within the magic and within her voice that both pains me and makes me hopeful.

"I do not wish for you to have to look upon me." My voice sounds strained, even to myself. I do not want to show her this weakness, but I do not know what else to do. I do not know what else to say. I feel broken down by watching her cry in that damned mirror for this long. I feel broken down by all these years of being cursed. "Please. For the moment, put on the blindfold and spare yourself."

I pause to allow Elle to consider my request. I can hear her sitting up in bed, the covers rustling as she does.

"I want to see you," she says, her voice soft but determined. "Will you let me see you?"

A deep sigh leaves me. I'm no longer willing to spend time discussing this with her. I need to be in the room with Elle, where I can speak to her. Where I can try to explain and hear what she is thinking. I cannot do either of those things if I am only watching her grieve through the mirror.

I open the door and take a few steps into her room. Shamed and enraptured by the hell of the curse and my image. Elle is sitting up in bed, just as I thought she would be.

Her eyes and cheeks are red, and her cheeks are streaked with tears. At some point it seems as though she braided her hair, but it is coming loose from the braid, and there is no ribbon to tie it off at the end. It is a mess, and she is beautiful.

Her eyes move over me as she takes me in. I know what she sees. It is the same thing I always see when I look in the mirror and the very thing I never wanted her to witness.

Elle's eyes trail down my body, then rise slowly back to my face. She is distraught, that is true, but her distress does not deepen when she looks at me.

That is strange. The beast makes a questioning sound inside of me. He does not know what it means when someone looks at him this way, as if he is *not* a beast.

I'm waiting for Elle's eyes to widen and for fear to consume her, but it doesn't.

Instead, the look on her face becomes soft and pleasing, as if she wants nothing more than to be at my side.

I should hesitate and approach cautiously, but it has been too long to force myself to do that. I cross her room in a few strides, sit beside her on the bed, and take Elle in my arms.

Her warmth is everything. She allows me to hold her, to comfort her. Her scent and soft curves are a soothing balm. For a moment there is peace within me if for no other reason than she allows me in her presence.

She slumps against me, burying her face in my shirt, her shoulders shaking with more tears. I pat her hair and drop kisses onto her head, wondering how one person can feel so much sadness. I would have thought she'd be out of tears, but she is not.

"It will be all right," I tell her, hoping she believes me.

"No, it will not." Elle lifts her head but does not pull away from me. "Who are you? The prince?"

Her question shocks me to my core. I am unable to answer her as she stares deep into my eyes. "You are both," she whispers, and her discovery causes her eyes to widen, but not like I'd imagined.

Silence descends for a moment and I can only admit the truth. "Yes, I am. I once was."

Her eyes narrow with confusion and I'm sure mine do as well.

"Prince...what is your name?" she asks, and it pains me to remember.

With haze clouding my judgment, I tell her, "My name is Henry."

She whispers the name I used to go by and my eyes close. A pain rushes through me, and I shush her. *Do not call me that,* I wish to tell her but the words fail me.

To my surprise, she confides in me. "I do not know what to do with these feelings."

"What feelings? Are you upset that I killed Lord Crawe? They were here to steal you away." I know I should not be condemning men for trying to do the same thing I did, but

I cannot help it. "If they had somehow found a way into the castle, they would have done everything in their power to take you back to the village and to kill me."

"I know that is what they would have done. And I am not sad that Lord Crawe is dead. I am happy he's dead. I have wanted men like him dead for longer than you know."

She leans her head on my shoulder, and I keep my arms around her.

"It is," Elle continues, "quite a different thing to see the others and to not know..." She's not able to finish.

I gather her close to my chest and smooth down her hair while the last of her tears run out of her eyes. It must have been a shock for Elle to see so many dead at one time, all by my hands.

Elle's shoulders finish shaking, and on her next breath, she lifts her face to mine and kisses me.

She kisses me as if she needs to in order to breathe. Her warm lips mold to mine and her chest presses to mine. *She kisses me.*

I go still, shocked, but then my body responds to hers as it has always done. I kiss her back, my heart unsteady at this contact. Elle is kissing me of her own volition. I have not demanded anything from her, and she is kissing me. It is a salty, tear-filled kiss, but it is a relief to us both.

When she pulls back, I run my knuckles down her cheek, reveling in touching her while I look into her eyes. It is so different from when she wore the blindfold. So much of her expressiveness is in her eyes, and it is a sin that I have not delved into the depths of her beauty like this before.

"I do not wish to harm." I take a breath, stroking my thumb over her cheek. Elle's skin is the softest I have ever felt. She is the most beautiful woman I have ever touched. I would steal her from her father's house a hundred times over and never be able to bring myself to regret it. "I did not want to kill them, Elle, and I do not want to harm anyone else who comes here. But I will not let them take you."

Elle's lip trembles. "But what of my father?" she questions, and I am thankful I have prepared an answer, although I do not know its truthfulness in all certainty. I'm fairly sure of it, but not entirely as the world becomes red when the beast takes control.

"I would never harm him," I tell her. "He is safe. He wasn't among them." She holds me tighter than before. Her gratitude is clinging to me.

I would lie a thousand times over to feel her touch forever. Although I pray that what I said is true. And if it's not, I pray she lives in peaceful ignorance. I need her to love me. Simply to survive, I need her to love me like this.

CHAPTER 27

ELLE

The beast kisses me, or rather the prince, I do not know which and I don't understand what my mind has done to see him how he is now and yet as he was...but I know he is both. And I know that I love him. His hand rises to my face and his other arm circles my back to draw me closer.

I'm a shattered mess, but he does not seem to care. He kisses me deeply, making soft sounds into the kiss of the likes I have not heard from him since the night I found myself in his bed. A deep primal need that's as intoxicating as the magic that surrounds the castle.

I don't even try to understand while he kisses me, his fingers stroking the side of my face and down my neck. It is no use when I have no wits about myself. I can feel his desire for me, and he must feel my desire for him, but I do not know if I can offer him that right now. I'm exhausted from crying for so long, and I am also exhausted by the relief I feel at having the beast here with me.

I know that sounds like it cannot be true, but I could almost fall asleep if he weren't kissing me like this. I would not have minded if he wanted to lie down on the pillows with me and sleep for a long time. He may need it as much as I do, after all that has happened and now that he allows me to see him.

Because in addition to seeing him with my own eyes, I am touching him, and my hands confirm what I feel. I cannot imagine that the beast's body is an illusion. It feels too real under my hands, and when I peek out from under my lashes to make sure the warm skin and the muscle and bone underneath my fingertips match what I see with my eyes, they are always correct. I have no reason to disbelieve them.

His eyes are the same...but at this moment he has the body of a man. Strong sharp features and a rugged yet charming look. He is both. How was that never shared in the lore? It is as if he can shift from one to the other. My heart beats wildly and the same feeling from the first night returns. A deep need to touch him and to be bound to him. As if our love was fated. As if nothing else matters.

I feel almost breathless from how tenderly he kisses me,

and how deeply.

It makes me dizzy to be kissed like this. The beast pulls away and looks into my eyes with curiosity. I put my hands to his face and feel his carved cheekbones. He flinches as if my touch pains him. I pull away, not wanting to stop him from loving me.

"I did not mean to hurt you."

"No? Does it not disturb you to see me like this?" he questions and then adds, "Knowing what I am?"

"No," I tell him honestly in a whisper, then lean in and offer him a gentle kiss. He closes his eyes for a few seconds, then opens them again, watching my face. "My prince."

With my words, the magic is broken, snapping right before my eyes.

He jerks away, getting from his feet and taking a step back from the bed. His sudden withdrawal shocks me, and I put a hand to my chest.

"Don't call me that," he orders, his voice sharp.

With my heart racing and my mind not understanding, I blink at the change in tone. He has ordered me to do many things, but this is the first time I have heard him speak to me in such pained anger.

"Is there something else I should call you?"

He narrows his eyes. "Call me what I am."

"You are a prince."

I'm only stating what is true. For most of my life, I believed the stories the villagers said about the beast. That he was a *beast* who was once a man but was cursed by a witch and turned into a creature like the world had never seen before. A dangerous creature who would kill anyone who tried to get a glimpse of him. And yet, here he is before me.

Those are just stories, as I have learned. The man before me is not a creature unlike any I have ever seen. The stories said that he was most like a wolf, but far too large to be defeated. That, too, was just a story. The man standing in the middle of my room, his hands at his sides and his face flushed from his anger, is a *man*.

Flesh like mine.

I have seen many men before, but I have never seen one as handsome as the prince.

The prince stares at me, his eyes sharp and his shoulders rising and falling as he breathes. Anger rises in him and though the magic in the castle tries, it cannot soothe the tension between us now.

"I'm not a prince," he growls, then strides across the room to the mirror. He jerks it on a sharp angle, the heavy weight of it nothing to him. "*Look.*"

Has he gone mad? Can he not see himself for who he is?

"I am looking." I dare to speak the truth, my words barely able to be spoken. I swallow thickly. "I have seen you." I glance in the mirror, but his reflection is just the same as the man I see standing in the room. There is nothing different about it.

"You are a man and a prince. And I have seen you as the beast as well." My heart races, the temperature in the room rising with the fear within me.

He looks into the mirror, a faint hope crossing his face and then falling away. Whatever he sees makes him bare his teeth and snarl at his reflection. I grip the sheets tighter, startled by his reaction.

"I am a *beast!*"

"You aren't." I get out of the bed, ignoring how tired my legs remain and cross to him, taking his hand in mine. He lets me do it, but he trembles with suppressed emotion. "You are a man. When I look at you, and when I look into the mirror, I see the same thing. A tall man, handsome, with—"

"Don't lie to me," he practically sneers and drops my hand.

With a step back, I move away from him, my body instinctively taking me away from danger.

I do not want him to think I am afraid of him, but I also do not want him to think I'm lying. He doesn't see what I see. How is that possible? I can see him clearly when I look at him, and his reflection is just as clear in the mirror.

The beast, who still looks every bit the prince, bares his teeth at me and lets out a growl of pure anger and pain. My heart drops, then begins to beat so intensely that I cannot breathe as I watch him change before my eyes. It takes me a few moments to realize what I'm feeling.

This is the first time I've been terrified of the beast. With both my hands raised, I whisper, "Please don't hurt me." And with shock and regret in his gaze, he runs from the room, more a beast than a man.

CHAPTER 28

THE PRINCE AND THE BEAST

In the tower, I sit before the rose and stare at it, practically unseeing, for too long before I manage to shake myself out of my thoughts and admit what sits before me.

The rose is nearly bare. Almost every petal has fallen from the stem, and they lay on the bottom of the cloche in a soft pile that would be nothing if it was not counting down the days I have left.

I close my eyes and hope for it to be different when I open them.

I heave myself out of the seat with a growl, my frustrations like a fire inside me. There's a mirror on one wall. It has been on the wall since before the curse, but I have long since stopped looking at it. What does it have to tell me? Nothing but to remind me that I am a beast. The rose was the only thing that mattered in this room.

In the mirror, I am unchanged. I am the frightening predator who stalks the woods, who tears at throats and roars in the night. My gaze drops to my hands, and the carved claws and brown fur are still there. Never leaving. How could she look at this and call me the prince?

"Nothing but the beast," I whisper.

"That is not what I see."

Elle's voice startles me, and I turn from the mirror to find her standing in the doorway to the tower room. She must have climbed to the room with soft footsteps, because I did not hear her approach.

Anger and disbelief fill me, turning my body hot and my muscles tense.

"You are not welcome here," I remind her in a harsh tone that does not seem to affect her. I have forbidden Elle from being here. She has always avoided the tower, and yet now she has chosen to follow me here. I do not know whether I am angry that I did not prevent her from climbing the stairs or angry that she has seen me in a moment of weakness.

This is weakness.

"I know," she says softly but doesn't move. Her head stays bowed, her eyes red rimmed and her hair in a messy braid. Her wide eyes stare back at me and her lips part, but she says nothing.

"What are you doing here?" I manage to keep my voice steady, but it is difficult.

Elle takes two small steps into the room, her head held high. I can tell that she is not feeling as brave as she looks. Her hands tremble slightly, but she clasps them together in front of her and tries to stop them from shaking.

"You are the prince," she says.

I turn away from her with a sound of disgust. "Do not look at me."

"I swear it!" Elle takes another step forward but stops when I give her a sharp look over my shoulder. "I do not see a beast! I only see you."

I look back down at my body. It is the body of a beast. It is not the body of the prince I was before I was cursed. I can hardly remember what I looked like. "You do not need to flatter me. I know I am a beast. And even if you deny that, I am *still* a beast for what I have done."

"I saw you as a beast," Elle says softly, her eyes determined. "I saw the beast that is in you, but in this moment...you are not him. You are the prince."

"The magic—"

"It is not the magic. I can see clearly. I feel you. I've touched your skin and kissed you. You have blue eyes and dark brown hair that falls to your shoulders. It is wavy but does not curl into ringlets. I can see you."

My stomach clenches. Elle is describing the man I once was, but that is impossible. I look into the mirror, bracing myself to see that I have changed.

I have not. The beast stares back at me. He has gold eyes and the face of a beast. There is no mistaking it, and certainly no confusing it for the man I used to be.

And Elle cannot know what I looked like before I was cursed. I tore all the portraits of me that existed in the castle to shreds years ago. Not a single one remains. They were too painful to look at, and when the beast was in control, he responded to that pain by doing whatever he could to destroy them. The canvases were no match for his claws.

I turn away from the mirror and meet Elle's eyes. If she is lying to me, it does not show on her face. She simply watches me as if her fear of me earlier was a mistake, and now she understands why I could not accept what she said.

I swallow, my throat dry. "How do you know what I once looked like?"

Elle's brow furrows. "I do not know what you mean."

"You have just described the man I was before the curse. That is not what I look like now. You are not seeing clearly."

She looks at me again, blinking as if to clear her vision, then waits a few more seconds.

Elle shakes her head. "I was not describing the way you used to look. I was describing the way you look now. The way you look at this moment, standing here in front of me.

As you are now."

I search for the beast inside of me. He is at peace, still, resting, but not gone. He is never going to be gone. I glance out the window at the night sky. The moon hangs heavy and bright. It's nearly the full moon. The days passed quickly after the new moon, and especially after the attack. At its sight, I feel the pull, both to the beast and to Elle. The magic is strong when the moon is full.

"What did the spell say?" Elle asks and as I return my sight to her, she is focused on the rose that is almost no more. "If you could tell me—"

If I told her, there would still be nothing she could do. That is not the nature of the spell. Suddenly the loneliness of the hours I have spent in the tower, watching the rose petals and making foolish wishes, as if they could change what is to come wraps around me. I feel every moment I have spent apart from Elle and how much of a waste it was, and I cannot control what I want from her. I do not care if it makes me weak.

"Please," I say, my voice rough. "Kiss me."

Elle moves toward me, her eyes soft and her hands already lifting to touch me. I am entranced all over again by how she comes to me without fear. This is a woman who has every right to fear me. She has seen me at my most dangerous, and still she followed me here to tell me that I do not look like a beast. Elle came here to tell me that she sees the prince I once was.

That is not possible. It can never be possible, but in her

eyes, I can see that she believes it. For that, I thank the magic.

Perhaps it does not matter what I look like. It has mattered to me a great deal since I lost the person I was before the curse. I knew the witch would not be kind, as she was too drunk on her own power when I came to her. She was able to hold the lives of all the villagers over my head, and there was no reason for her to show mercy, and she did not.

For such a long time, I have thought of myself as suffering a punishment that was almost as final as death. The villagers who had once sent me away to bargain for their lives feared me and hated me, and it was because they did not see me as the prince.

They saw me as the beast I have seen in the mirror every time I brought myself to look into one. The villagers and I have this in common. We both know what we are looking at.

So perhaps it is a miracle that Elle does not see that. Perhaps it is an act of magic. Perhaps it is a kind of mercy that I never thought was possible. As she walks to me, I am willing to believe it, and it does not matter that I might only let myself believe her because there is almost no time left for anything else.

What does my reflection matter now? If I never look in a mirror again, I can pretend that Elle is right, and I will not have to pretend for very long.

She is almost within reach, her hand inches from mine, a gentle smile on her face, when there is a noise in the stairwell.

I hear this one with all of my senses. I hear the scrape of a boot on the stone stairs, and a *thump*, as if the person climbing the stairs has lost his balance. I can smell the presence of another human being in the castle. *Impossible,* my mind cries. I have spent so long keeping them out that it is *impossible* for another man to be here. And I can feel the change in the air on my skin.

"Elle?" a voice calls.

Elle whips her head toward the sound. "Father?"

The beast leaps from his slumber, seizes control, and lets out a roar of rage that shakes the entire tower. The stones tremble beneath my feet. Everything goes red. My skin turns to fire as he fights for control, and I don't know how I can possibly hold the beast back.

CHAPTER 29

ELLE

I am mere steps away from the prince when he changes, morphing from the man I saw when he came to my room to comfort me, and the same man I saw just moments ago, into the *beast.* I knew it to be true. That he was both. But to see him, his skin shredding to become thick fur and his back arching, his claws and teeth bared. It's a fright to behold.

"Please," I manage. "You promised." I barely get out before the beast is before me.

My heart races but I try to stay calm. It's not the first time I've been in his presence. The swing comes back to me. He must've been the beast then.

He is tall and wolflike, his teeth sharp and his eyes gold.

His dark brown hair and blue eyes are gone. His muscles are corded and hard, pressing at his clothes, splitting the fabric.

As his gaze turns from me to the stairs, he roars, and my instincts betray me.

I let out a scream of terror, unable to swallow it, so loud it hurts my throat. I have never *seen* such a creature, and I have certainly never felt such a creature touch me. Those hands would not feel like the prince's hands. Those hands have claws, like a wolf, and they are razor sharp and deadly. Those teeth are what bit me.

The mark of the beast.

Footsteps climb faster up the stairwell as my heart races.

"Elle!" My father sprints up the stairs, calling out my name, but stops dead at the sight of the beast. He falls backward, hitting the ground hard, his elbow cracking on the stone.

For a moment I feel nothing but panic and a pure, unavoidable fear. No matter how many times I blink, the beast stays a beast. He does not turn back into the prince.

But then I blink once more, and there is a change. I can see the prince at the heart of the beast. I can see the beast whose form he has taken. It is as if I can see them both at once, changing between forms so quickly that I cannot make sense of him.

With a growl, the beast moves to the stairs, and I try to stop him. Grabbing at his fur but it's no use.

I do not know if the beast can hear me. I do not know if

he knows what the prince promised.

"Not my father! Please!" I scream.

My father climbs to his feet and rushes at the beast, who bats him away like he is a child or an insect. He falls back to the ground clutching his head. There is blood, but I cannot take my eyes off the beast for long enough to see to my father's wound.

"Father don't! Please!" I hold a hand up to my father. "Please don't fight him!" I cry out, tears leaking from the corner of my eyes.

"I love him! Please!" I scream and I'm not certain which person, man or beast, my father or the prince, I'm pleading to.

"Please stop!" I call out and the beast pauses. My father calls my name like a question. "Elle?"

The beast looks back at me, I hold his gaze. "My father. Please," I beg him and with a whine, the beast's head lowers, and I feel as though he understands.

"Please," I beg again as he takes a step back, giving me a path to my father.

This tower room is too small to make any escape. My father groans at my feet and I crouch down, touching him. There is blood on the floor from the wound at his head. I murmur at him to be still, but I can hardly hear my own voice. I need to find the wound so I can stop the bleeding.

It was a mistake to take my eyes off the beast.

He roars, the sound hurting my ears, and it seems to rattle

the stone beneath my feet. I see his shadow loom over us, and then my father scrambles upright.

"Father, no!"

He does not hear my cry. Once again my father rushes at the beast with nothing but his bare hands, but the beast roars into his face. My father stumbles back, falling in front of me.

"Elle," he says, and puts up one arm to try to defend us.

The beast swipes one enormous paw across my father's body and sends him flying toward the wall. My father slams into it with a terrible thump and crumbles to the floor of the tower, unmoving.

"Father, no!"

My feet don't want to get underneath me, but I force myself upright and run to my father. I place myself between him and the beast. I do not know if he is alive. I cannot bend down to see if he is breathing. I send up a prayer to anyone who will listen to let my father survive this. He does not deserve to die like this.

I put up both hands as the beast stalks across the tower toward me, his claws and teeth bared, growling through his teeth. He is so much taller this way, and the panic in me grows until I think there may be no hope.

The moment he is close enough, I place both hands on his shoulders and push as hard as I can. I am not strong enough to stop him from moving, but I put all the strength I have into holding him back.

"Please, stop! Please," I cry, hoping to be heard over his growls. They are threatening noises, like something out of a nightmare. But he doesn't hurt me. He does not swipe at me. I do not know what will happen next, because I saw the beast enter a similar fury the night the castle was attacked. He must feel this is the same.

Thoughts fly in my mind and I hold onto the beast, wrapping my arms around him. I whisper for him to stop. I beg him. "He's not going to hurt you," I continue. "My father isn't trying to hurt you, I promise. He would not have come here to attack you. Please, stop."

My tears linger in his fur and the beast's form rises and falls with heavy breaths. He's quiet beneath me. With the world quiet around me, I dare to pull back. I dare to loosen my grip and get a look at the beast.

For a single moment, the beast's eyes change. A flash of the prince's blue eyes peeks out from behind the gold. That color is gone in an instant, but it was there.

"I see you," I whisper, my voice shaking because my heart will not slow. "I *see* you," I repeat, hoping against hope that he will hear me and understand.

The beast cocks his head on an angle, his eyes gold again. There is no sign that the blue was ever there, but in the beast's eyes, confusion flares. He is no longer growling, and his shoulders do not press as hard against my hands. The beast blinks, staring into my eyes. His head lowers and he presses himself into me again. As if a dog wanting to be held. I hold him tightly and pray this will be enough.

"Please," I whisper, begging again. I need to breathe, but I cannot force my lungs to work to calm myself. My heart will not slow until I can make sure my father is all right, and I am terrified that if I wait too long, he will not make it.

The beast eases away from me. I keep my hands up, trying to signal to him that he does not need to fear me and that he does not need to come after my father. There is nothing the man can do to him. He has not made a sound since he fell to the floor and could not harm the beast even if he wanted to.

Then he changes. Right before my eyes. From beast to prince. Relief and disbelief are a maddening thing. The magic and the castle, the last weeks of my life, they are a fantasy that is too fantastical to ever be believed. The prince was never gone.

The transformation is difficult for my eyes to take in. His body seems to blur, shifting even as I watch. There's cracking of bones and the torn clothes fall. I do not know where to look because all of him is changing at once. He is bared to me. Eventually his features smooth out into the man he was when I entered the tower. His chest heaves as if he cannot breathe, and his expression is anguished. His blue eyes shine in the moonlight that comes through the tower, and his hands ball into fists at his sides. He no longer has claws, but I can see the tension in him. The prince may have the form of the man, but he still carries the pain of the beast.

He bares his teeth, gritting them as if to master his feelings.

I take a deeper breath to regain control of my own. I can't help but to hold him, to wrap my arms around him. He barely holds me back but when I pull away from him, he searches my eyes for something, but I cannot know what.

"My father—" I begin.

"He should not have come here," the prince says, his voice taut with the words. I can hear his anger in them and perhaps fear. His gaze lingers on my father, and he says, "What have I done?"

CHAPTER 30

THE PRINCE AND THE BEAST

E lle watches me with bright, wary eyes and does not seem to know what to do. And as I stare at the old man lying in the corner of the tower, I do not know either. She trembles on her feet, her face flushed, and her hair mussed as if it was tousled by the magic.

"He..." She swallows, dropping her hands to the front of her skirts.

I go to him before she can finish. The back of my hand to his mouth. Relief floods through me as warmth graces my skin. "He's breathing."

"Father," she cries out and rushes past me to him. She cradles his face in her hands, and I feel shame and agony. I made her a promise I knew I would not be able to keep. For the beast is brutal and knows nothing of promises.

"Will he be all right?" I dare to ask her, knowing all too well how much he means to her.

With glassy eyes she looks up at me. "He'll be okay, I think. I just need him to wake."

I answer, my voice rough. "I could have killed him."

"But you didn't." Elle smiles weakly. "You are not only a beast. You are also the prince, and when it mattered most, you knew that."

I do not dare glance down at my body. I do not know if what my own eyes see matters anymore.

"Please"—she looks up at me—"will you help me get him to bed?"

I can only nod, not understanding her demeanor. She is not angry or afraid. For a moment a spark of hope goes through me.

"What do you see when you look at me now?" I ask.

Her eyes travel over my body but quickly return to my face. "You are a tall, handsome man with wavy dark brown hair and blue eyes. I can *see* your blue eyes." Elle stands and leaving her father for only a moment, she steps closer as if to make sure they are blue. She nods to herself, her shoulders relaxing. "I can see you just as you were when I came into the tower. That is not how you look when you...when you are the beast. You are taller, with gold eyes, and you have a wolf's features." She looks down my chest and then blushes.

"Your clothes have torn," she tells me, though I know they have. The beast tears them from me. It is not the first time. "When you...change, they tear."

"When I change?"

"Your body...I wish you could see what I see."

That is what I have seen in the mirror every day since the witch laid the curse on me. I almost step to the mirror to prove Elle wrong, but after all that has happened and with almost all the petals from the rose fallen off the stem, I no longer want to look. The beast has retreated. He is not fully gone, but he seems to recognize that this man from the village—Elle's father—is alone and harmless. Even if he wanted to steal her away, he could not do it. Even if he wanted to hurt me, he could not do that either. He tried to fight me with his bare hands. That is no way to confront a beast such as myself.

"You do not have the beast's features now," Elle says, even more determinedly. "You are the prince."

My mind reels. I put a hand to my hair and draw it away before I can truly register what I feel under my palm.

"When I touch you," Elle says softly, "I feel the shape of the man. You have the body of the prince whenever we are together. I would know if I kissed you when you had the form of a beast, and I never have. I know you see something else when you look into the mirror, but that is not what I see. A beast is not all I have come to know at the castle. You are not just the beast. You are both."

I open my mouth, but I cannot think of the words I need to reply. Exhaustion betrays my strength.

"Let me help," I offer and kneel by her father. "He is a foolish man to come here." It is then that I look up to the window and out to the gate to see it closed, and no one else with him. "I could have killed him."

"You didn't."

I almost killed Elle's father. If I had not heard her voice at that moment, it would have been nothing for me to end his life. The beast considered him a threat to both of us, as he would anyone who breached the castle walls and came inside and climbed the highest floor of this remote tower.

"I cannot always control the beast."

Elle kneels down beside me next to her father, shaking his shoulder gently. I swallow thickly, hoping the old man will be all right.

"Father," she says. "Father, it's me. Wake up."

Her father lets out a low groan.

"Father," Elle says, more insistently. "Wake up. It's time to wake up."

"My head." Her father grunts and his body stirs.

"I know. I will help you."

There is a strange fear that grips me. The unknown of Elle knowing more of me than I do. And of her father being here. Surely he will take her away. And I do know that I can stop him.

I watch her help her father to an upright position, leaning against the wall. Elle pushes herself into his arms and they embrace for a few minutes, his eyes squeezed closed and his arms tight around his daughter. There is a trickle of blood down his face, either from one of my claws or from hitting the stone wall. Guilt and shame run through me.

It is only by a miracle that the man lives. The beast has never shown mercy before.

Finally, Elle straightens up again and looks into her father's eyes. She brushes his hair out of his face, whispering to him. It is then I gather enough wits about me to cover myself with a shred of the trousers.

With a noise behind me, clothes gather themselves in a pile and I accept the magic's offering. They appear from nothing and are far better than the strips of fabric. I allow them to dress me as I do every morning. It dawns on me the number of times I've thought it was the beast who tore them. I glance at my hand and as I turn it, my palm seems to be more like I once was.

"Father," she says, and my beauty distracts me.

Bandages and a large bowl of water float in through the door, and Elle accepts them, then sets about cleaning her father's wound. He's already talking to her, though he winces when he turns his head, so I think the wound is worse than it appears. Elle dabs the blood away with a wet cloth and bandages the wound. Then she holds his hand in hers, and the two of them speak to each other.

Their hands...

If she is right...

I place a hand to my chest and allow myself to feel what is there.

It feels like the chest of a man. My pulse speeds up, but I leave my hand on my chest. I am not imagining it. The beast feels different because he is more than a man. There is a wolflike creature within him as well.

Hardly breathing, I lift my hand to my face.

It is the first time in so many years that I have felt the face of a prince under my fingertips that I have to swallow a gasp. I keep my face turned away from the mirror, because I do not want the magic of the curse to interfere. Am I truly what I once was?

Across the room, Elle helps her father to his feet. "What were you thinking, Father?"

He embraces her again. "I had to know if you were all right. I could not spend the rest of my days wondering what had happened to you."

"I am well," she says, smiling at him. "I promise I am well, Father. But you should not be seen coming to or from the castle. No one else can know I am here."

They pause at the top of the steps, and Elle's father looks over her head at me. I rise to my feet, keeping a hand on the table for balance.

"Who is this?"

"The prince," she answers.

"Prince?" His eyes narrow and then widen in awe. "You're alive? You're...unchanged?" he questions and my heart races. He sees me as I once was, too? His voice hushes. "Where is the beast?"

"He is both, Father," she tells him, and I stare in wonder. He stares at me, leery and unsure of what Elle's said.

"Let's get him to a room," I offer.

"Thank you," Elle murmurs and I reach out, bracing the old man's arm and he lets me. More than that, he thanks me as well.

I lead them down the stairs and to a room that hasn't been used in decades, letting her say her goodbyes in privacy at the entrance of the room. Elle steps out and closes the door behind her.

Quietly, I lead her down the hall, my mind reeling and a new feeling coming over me. It is just the two of us now.

"When he is well, I will send him home."

I only nod in agreement.

"He can tell the villagers I am not here, and there is no one here but magic."

"That would be wise," I tell her.

"Perhaps he could return...and stay at times," she says like it's a question.

A moment passes and I attempt to see what she sees. "Perhaps," I answer and then ask, "Would that make you happy?"

"I would like that," she says softly and then her wide eyes reach mine. "It would make me happy to have company."

"But you will stay."

Elle nods, and her eyes drop to the floor. "I will not leave, but I would love his company."

"I will see to it that he is welcomed," I answer, more than anything grateful for her desire to stay.

"I am sorry for causing him pain," I tell her.

Elle does not answer. She looks at the floor at our feet. I wait as long as I can, but it is only a few moments before I need to see her eyes. I take her chin in my hand and tip her face up.

"Do you forgive me?" I ask.

Slowly, Elle nods.

I put my other hand to my chest, bracing myself for the honesty I know I must give to Elle. "I may look like the prince. I may...see myself as the prince. But I can still feel the beast inside."

Elle does not pull away. She steps closer to me, putting her hands on my waist. "Perhaps it is something you can control."

"I do not know that I can. I only know what the curse said."

"What is the curse?" she asks me.

"She said if I did not find my fate, when the last petal falls I would be nothing but the beast."

"But it's fallen," she whispers.

"What?" I question, not believing she knows what she's said.

"I saw it…in the tower. I saw the last petal fall."

My heart races as I leave her in the hall, striding to the tallest tower. My hands clench beside me and my emotions tear through me. The beast is still with me, I can feel him stir. Breathlessly, I get to the final step and fall slowly to my knees as I stare at the cloche. The rose is no more.

Is it over? Is the curse no more? Deep inside of me, I feel him stir. The beast.

"Prince!" she cries out and her voice echoes up the tower. "Henry!" she cries my name.

My name. It's then I look in the mirror. My reflection betrays me. No longer a beast. My body sags against the frame. "The curse…"

"Henry." Elle's voice is calm and breathless, and I turn to see her, standing before me.

And all I can think is that she is my fate.

"I love you," I tell her and practically crawl to meet her halfway. She collapses in my arms.

"I love you," she tells me and then kisses me fiercely. "You see yourself, don't you?" she murmurs as she pulls away, both of her hands on my face. "You see what I see."

The magic stirs around us, a thick fog leaving the window, and I know then it is not over.

"Henry, do you see that you are the prince?" she asks me,

hope filling her eyes. The nearly full moon shines brightly down upon her face. I've never seen so much beauty as the way she looks at me.

All I can say is, "I love you."

Epilogue

Elle

We go out to the yard together, both of us bundled in the finest winter clothes I have ever seen. The magic of the castle has provided me with a beautiful, thick, fur-lined, hooded cloak to keep out the cold. The dress I wear underneath is soft, yet sturdy enough to keep me warm. I even have leather boots, also lined with fur that is so luxurious that it feels as though I am walking on a plush indoor rug even as we cross the frost-covered grass.

Tilting my chin up, I look at the clear blue sky, only to have snowflakes land on my eyelashes. This is the first snowfall since I arrived at the beast's castle, and I find myself delighted by it. I always loved the beginning of winter as a girl, though less so as the years went by and it only meant I was in danger of being cold.

Now I am the safest I have ever been from sharp winds. There is a castle to protect me, a prince who lives there, and magic to care for us both. We will be warm all winter, and I can feel the old delight again just as I once did.

It's the start of my happily ever after.

"It is snowing!" I tell the beast, who follows at my side, my hand in his arm. "Look!"

A smile grows as I catch a snowflake on the tip of my nose, and he rumbles a laugh. "If it is snowing, then we should not be outside." It's a sound I've grown to love. A sound I hear more and more with each passing day. Especially now that my father stays with us and the rumors he's spread are now told as truths: an heir to the prince returned and slaughtered the beast.

With that side of him tamed, we are safe. Although the village still fears the magic. We've had visitors and every time I can feel his anxiousness, but not once has the beast betrayed him. The full moon is not a night we have guests though, as that is the night that calls to the beast the most. It is the new moon that the appetite for the prince is most needy. I find myself drawn to my husband most then as well. I glance down at the ring on my finger. One day we may have a grand wedding, but for now, his vows of love spoken late at night to love me forever are all I need.

"I am warm. Are you not?" I ask.

"I'm warm," he admits, and gives me a look that seems to mean that he is warm because he is with me and not because of his fine clothes.

He holds his hand out and I give him mine to hold. The first kiss on the crook of my neck sends a smoldering need through me.

The moment he pulls back I kiss his cheek, his stubble rough against my lips. The pull between us turns hotter. My attraction for him grows more and more with each passing day.

The prince changes direction, taking me behind a large evergreen that grows near the castle wall. His touch is still warm because we have only been outside for a few minutes, and his mouth is even hotter as he kisses me, bracing me against the wall and pushing up my skirts so that he can find his way between my legs and stroke me there.

I have come once already by the time he unlaces his trousers and thrusts his cock inside me. My lips part with a silent cry of ecstasy. If I had ever escaped from the castle, I would have craved the way he fills me and the possessive touch he uses to brace me against the wall. His body is so hot and his need is so all-encompassing that I do not even feel the cool of the bricks as he fucks me ruthlessly. He is the perfect lover.

He kisses the side of my neck, his powerful hands holding me in place, and all I have to do is hold him and take my pleasure from his body.

He finds his release with a growl at the same time I find mine, then covers my mouth with his and kisses me until I have to pull away to catch my breath. He lets me down carefully, placing my boots in the snow, and shakes out my skirts so that they fall around my legs.

"There. Now you do not look as if you have been ravished in the snow," he proclaims, catching his own breath.

"Thank you," I tell him, although he leans down to kiss me before I've finished. My legs are weak, but my prince pulls me closer to his side. He leads me to the swing that I sat on so long ago and brushes the thin layer of snow off the seat.

I sit on it, feeling like a princess. He bends down and kisses my neck, then pulls my cloak into place. He has kissed the spot where the scars from his teeth still remain, but all I feel now is the pleasure of his lips meeting my body. It doesn't matter where he kisses me. Every brush of his lips is like being warmed by the fireplace.

The prince steps behind me, taking the ropes of the swing in his hands, then pushes me lightly on my back. I do not want to swing too high. I want to stay where my prince is, never out of his reach. But it is such a simple pleasure, to be on a swing and remember how the magic lured me to him what seems like an eternity ago.

He pushes me again, and a small laugh escapes me simply from his touch. It is the hand of a prince that gives me a gentle push, not the hand of the beast. Although the beast will return, I have taught him that the prince still lives, and he is mine. I love them both for what they are. Mine to love. Their fate.

The magic of this place, and of the curse, is powerful indeed. But love is more so.

THE WITCH

The prince seems to love her devoutly. His fated mate. The snow does not bother us as we watch, and Elle and Prince Henry do not give any sign that they know they are being observed.

They are in love. That is plain to see even without any magical ability. It is in the way he looks at her, and she at him. She doesn't fear the beast when he returns either. This is a good sign. "There is hope after all," my sister murmurs and I nod in agreement.

"What shall we call him?" I say to the closest of my sisters.

She watches with narrowed eyes, her quick mind working. The prince brings Elle to a stop and helps her to her feet. They continue their walk around the yard, staying close to one another.

"Werebeast?" my sister offers.

"Werewolf," I suggest.

"Our first of many?" she asks.

"We must." My expression may have been light, watching the prince and Elle, the first successful pairing from the magic, but it was not carefree. Now is not the time for losing track of what we must do. "There are dark forces brewing, and we must do what must be done. Time is not on our side," I remind them.

There is no one else to do what must be done. So often, men and kings believe they are the people who will keep their kingdoms safe, but that is rarely the case. Most men—even kings—do not have the knowledge that is required to fight off forces like the ones that will soon descend on us. On all the world. For beasts in the night are plenty, and the sorcerers have conjured a darkness that sends the coldest of chills to wake me from the nightmares of what will be.

My sister chews at her bottom lip, thinking this over as she watches the prince and Elle. He has gathered snow in his hands to make a snowball, but when he throws it at her, she runs and he misses. She throws one back and it hits his arm. There is so little time left for games like these. They will live to have their happily ever after, as the time of mortals is so short. But their children's children will see the terrors that have been foretold.

"We will need to see what becomes of their children," I remind them.

"How many beasts will it take?"

I take a deep breath, releasing it slowly. "As many as we can. The prince was only the first werewolf. It will take centuries, my sister. Centuries of pain will fall before there will be peace."

"Off to Shadow Falls then?" My sister questions, gathering her cloak, satisfied with what's become of her making.

"All too ready to cast again?" I ask her and all of us smile wickedly. "To Shadow Falls," I whisper in a hiss. And with the flick of my wrist, we leave The Prince and His Beauty...for now.

About the Author

Thank you so much for reading my romances. I'm just a stay at home Mom and an avid reader turned Author and I couldn't be happier.

I hope you love my books as much as I do!

More by Willow Winters
www.willowwinterswrites.com/books

This is the Artist Rendition

Artwork by Elizianna the One

You can find each edition at

www.willowwinterswrites.com/books